PRAISE FOR *THE*
MISFORTUNES

"A spellbinding symphony of suspense and sorrow. Embark on a voyage to *The Island of Small Misfortunes*, where ghosts and mysteries intertwine in a tale that will haunt your thoughts long after the final page."

—Sara Crocoll Smith, editor of the award-winning *Love Letters to Poe* anthologies

"Jackson Kuhl performs a literary séance in *The Island of Small Misfortunes*, summoning forth the ghosts of America's past, complete with all the mystery, fraud, and greed of a bygone era in which spiritualists were indistinguishable from the charlatans on Wall Street."

—Marc E. Fitch, author of *Dead Ends* and *Boy in the Box*

"Part gothic mystery and part weird tale, *The Island of Small Misfortunes* is a voyage into the uncanny like no other."

—Alistair Rey, author of *The Art of Ghost Writing*

THE ISLAND OF SMALL MISFORTUNES

Jackson Kuhl

Regal House Publishing

Published by
Regal House Publishing, LLC
Raleigh, NC 27605
All rights reserved

ISBN -13 (paperback): 9781646035380
ISBN -13 (epub): 9781646035397
Library of Congress Control Number: 2024935077

Cover images and design by © C. B. Royal

Regal House Publishing, LLC
https://regalhousepublishing.com

Printed in the United States of America

For John Hunter Kuhl

1

The first time Sequoia Owen met his uncle Preston was in New York, when his mother brought Sequoia and his sister Patricia, then just an infant, to the St. Nicholas Hotel for lunch. His uncle treated him politely, even kindly, but largely ignored the children. Preston's attention focused solely on their mother.

"You look like a tree that hasn't been watered," he said to her. She was Preston's older sister.

"Virginia isn't *friendly* to northerners," Sequoia remembered her saying. "But Charles's business is doing well. Where we are, the war barely touched."

"I can tell you're miserable. You and the children should return to Connecticut."

"You mean well but don't be absurd—I cannot leave him. Where would we even live?"

"On the island. At least to begin with."

"We'd have to be out by the fall. Then where?"

"I could make improvements to the house. Stay there as long as you want."

His uncle turned to Sequoia then and said, "You have a cousin about your age named Jacob. How would you like to meet him? You could spend every summer with him, swimming and sailing and climbing rocks."

"Preston, don't," said his mother. "The island isn't a good place for children."

Even if he didn't remember the words exactly right, the tension of the conversation impressed itself into Sequoia's memory, sitting there, small in his chair, in the sprawling dining room, the silver clattering on china. He recalled his uncle with unease, trying to break apart his family. And something about an island.

The second time Sequoia met his uncle was at his mother's funeral.

Uncle Preston traveled alone; to Sequoia, his aunt and cousins were yet hypotheticals, names mentioned softly by his mother whenever his father wasn't around. Upon his arrival at the church, Preston approached Sequoia's father, by then too sick to stand, and for a moment both men appraised each other with flinty eyes. Neither offered his hand.

"You have my condolences, Charles."

"Thank you, Preston," said Sequoia's father. And that was the extent of their interaction, the most words either man had spoken to each other in the better part of four decades—no rapprochement, no reconciliation in the presence of shared tragedy. Only vendettas sheathed for a day.

Once the casket had been lowered and the mourners turned to disperse, Preston made a beeline for Sequoia. Both men apologized for the other's loss.

"I want you to know," said Preston, "that whatever bitterness lies between me and Charles, it does not extend toward you and your sisters." Neither Patty nor Mary were present; both had married and moved west.

"You have my gratitude for that," said Sequoia. "You know, I possess fond recollections of that afternoon together at the St. Nicholas." Which was a fib, the memory little more than a cognizance of a vaguely ominous mustachioed stranger and Sequoia fiddling with his fork, pushing the oysters around in their shells.

Preston said he remembered that day clearly. "If you should ever travel north to New York, please stop by our townhouse. Or better yet—come spend a few weeks at the summer house in Connecticut. It was built by your grandfather."

"I would very much like that."

His uncle nodded and said nothing. To Sequoia it seemed as if he was trying to muster the right words, sentiment not coming easily for him. "I regret the war took my sister from me, long before death did," he said finally. "I wish to repair the wound as best I can."

"The summer home," said Sequoia. "Is that the place on an island?"

Preston's face brightened. "You remember. Yes— on Todeket. Among the Thimbles."

They spoke a few more moments but from the corner of his eye Sequoia could see his father struggling to rise from his chair, so after excusing himself, he went to assist. When he looked again, his uncle was gone.

With his mother passed and his father gravely infirm, Sequoia retired from the merchant service to devote the next eighteen months caring for him and his business affairs. Growing up along the banks of the Chesapeake in eastern Virginia, he'd always loved the water, and his career had been his second choice for getting to sea. His father explicitly denied the navy to him, for reasons never articulated but obvious in light of the family's history.

When the end came, Sequoia inherited a small amount of money and sold his father's business. Most of these profits he invested along with his saved earnings.

He immediately lost everything in the crash of '96.

The worst part of it was the brokers and advisers seemed as mystified by the loss as he was, and too late Sequoia realized they possessed as much insight into the inner workings of the economy as does a pig into Sunday supper. What hope then does the common man have of divining sheep's intestines if the priests in their temples were just as befuddled? There was nothing biologic in a machine, Sequoia realized; it was all gears and stacks and black smoke, serving only to tear off the digits and limbs of men if their attention should drift for even an instant.

The loss hung over him, a great cloud in a darkening sky. For years his luck was that of most men's, vacillating between the two poles so that Sequoia's life traveled an equatorial course overall. But then something happened and he crossed some latitude; or, as he at times imagined, some ague infected him in a foreign port. What began on board the ships spread like a contagion on land, taking first his love, then his parents, and finally his money.

Seeing then no reason why he should sweat at labor when the entire nation was run by card sharps and riverboat gamblers, Sequoia cast about for ideas that would preserve his comfort indefinitely. Only fools earned their incomes by work, he now perceived—wise men were owed their livings by America, God, and McKinley. Then he recalled his uncle's invitation to visit him in New York.

Sequoia also remembered a peculiar fact about his aunt.

Years before while in France, Sequoia had a business notion which, whenever it floated to the top of his mind, slowly convinced him of its marketability. So with his last remaining dollars, Sequoia constructed a working prototype and filed a patent with the office in Washington. There his progress halted, for he had no money to further develop or promote his conception. His epistolary hand stretched toward his uncle, in the roundabout hope that by ingratiating myself into his mother's family, Sequoia could obtain funding, if not an allowance, to invest in his creation which, if successful, would allow him to spend his remaining days easily. If it was unsuccessful, well—by that time Sequoia intended to sit high in his uncle's estimation.

Preston Wescott responded agreeably and invited him to their summer house on Todeket Island for the first weekend in August. No other details were forthcoming, but also neither was a date stipulated for Sequoia's departure. If circumstances went well, Sequoia imagined he might be able to pass the rest of the warm months rested and well fed at his uncle's expense. He sharply remembered that invitation offered to his mother to live at the island house indefinitely.

His train arrived late to town, and the station master informed Sequoia it would be impossible to catch a ferry to the island until morning. He found a room at the Indian Point House, and late the next morning arrived at the public landing where a harassed ferryman checked and double-checked the lines securing his steam launch. A woman stood on the dock, as straight and foreboding as Mephistopheles apparated in a cloud of brimstone, a pentagram of cases and parcels stacked around her by a dutiful valet.

"Looks like a breeze-up on its way, Mrs. Irving," said the ferryman to her. He gestured toward the gunmetal clouds rolling from the northeast.

Mrs. Irving waved away this news as if it was a housefly. "Do you think we can make it before the storm begins?"

The ferryman squinted skyward in a demonstration of courtesy. "Hard to say. It might be best to wait it out at the coffeehouse until after. Or you could ask one of the other ferrymen."

Yet nearby those men busied themselves furling and tying the sails of their catboats, refusing any eye contact. The pilot's launch was the only steamboat at the dock.

"What a bother. I'd much prefer to be at the house and unpack. It isn't raining yet." She turned to the servant. "Rutger, load my bags into the boat."

"Yes, ma'am." Rutger the valet jumped to it.

And so did Sequoia, joined by the reluctant ferryman, who found himself pressed into traveling into the oncoming storm with two separate fares. Once the passengers and Mrs. Irving's many boxes were stowed, the ferryman freed the mooring lines from the piles, stepped aboard, and took his seat by the tiller. He turned the handle to engage the propeller and they cast off.

The water close to the mainland had yet to grow rough as they passed Wheeler Island, small but steep, with its house perched high above them. The breeze against their faces carried a coolness of rain. Sequoia kept up a chatter with the ferryman, eager to learn as much as possible about the islands, and the latter responded, naming each island they passed, commenting on the fresh coat of paint sported by a house or a dock in obvious disrepair.

Mrs. Irving was less communicative, and for the whole voyage sat with one hand clamping her straw hat to her head. The Irvings' summer house lay on Money Island.

"To which island did you say you're headed?" she asked Sequoia.

"Todeket, on the southern edge."

"Oh," she said with a strange expression. For the rest of the journey she didn't speak to him or even glance his way.

The Thimbles numbered three-hundred sixty-five, one for every day of the year according to the salts loitering over their glasses at the Stony Creek saloon, which might even be true if an accountant enumerated every boulder breaking above the surface at ebb tide. Of these, only thirty-two Thimbles amounted to acreage enough for houses, and some of those little more spacious than the gap between front and back doors. They reached like phalanges into the Sound, digits submerged with only the knuckles above water. On a chart a straight line could be drawn between Outer Island and Horse Island and Pot Island and so on, with the odd bare heads of rock between them, all the way back to town. The other islands roughly lined up likewise. Between these rows were channels of water, smooth and glassy when calm but now beginning to jump under the growing wind.

As they steamed, the rain remained an unfulfilled threat. They weaved between a number of expensive-looking sailboats riding at anchor, and the ferryman explained, without elaboration, that they belonged to the Knickerbockers.

To their left they passed a proud three-story mansion perched on a mound of rocks—"Cut-in-Two," said the ferryman—while to their right lay a narrow splinter dominated by a flat house and a long lawn—"East Crib." The sea turned choppier. They crossed another channel and banked starboard. In minutes Money Island slid off their port-rail side, rows of cottages atop immense blocks of granite, grass and trees sprouting from the seams between them.

The ferryman followed Money's shoreline, the sky a deep gray and the wind pushing the stern like a theater usher's hand on their elbow. The night before at the saloon, Sequoia heard a common joke about Money Island: it was the poorest of the Thimbles because none of the residents could afford their own island, so instead they had to suffer neighbors.

Sequoia watched the water beside them, judging its color, and the ferryman kept them well away from the paler greens and browns that suggested stone lurking beneath. There were no beaches in the Thimbles, only granite, pink above the high-water mark and gray below. Piloting through the islands and the many almost-isles was the work of half memory, half intuition, and when he felt sure, the ferryman arced toward the dock on the western shore.

There were a half-dozen ferrymen in the Thimbles, most of them sailing from Indian Point and a few from Flying Point, all in semi-friendly competition with one another. Only part of their jobs involved shuttling the summer residents from the mainland to their island houses. Most often they worked as gofers, responding when an islander hung a red flag from his dock, a request for milk or bread or some other necessity from town, which a ferryman then retrieved like a trained hound. If he didn't, another man would.

Their pilot didn't bother to tie up at Money, merely idled beside the dock. Rutger helped Mrs. Irving step out. Sequoia handed the packages to him, each so featherlight they could've contained goose-down pillows. The cargo unladed, Rutger pushed heavily on the bow to launch the steamboat away. The ferryman reversed into deeper water, the tiller sharply pushed away from him, then shifted the propeller forward and pointed the prow south.

At that moment the leaves of the island trees turned over to show their petticoats like can-can dancers. A wall of rain collapsed on them. The suddenness of it was like a hangman pulling the lever of the trap, the water plummeting with all its weight behind it, and Sequoia rocked on his bench from the hammering upon the wooden cockpit roof.

The ferryman steamed southward around the tip of Money and cut nearly due east across the bow of Johnson Island, a pile of rocks barely above the waterline and fitted with a single shack. Rivers sluiced off the roof and soaked them both. Just as they hooked northward into the adjacent channel, Sequoia heard a shout above the wind. For an instant the rain broke, and as if through heavy closing drapes he saw a wave lift a small skiff and flip it like a playing card, the sailor spilling into the water. Then the rain fell again and the vision melted.

The blood inside Sequoia drained to his feet—he couldn't take a ten-minute ferry without calamity. He leapt up and pointed. *"Man overboard."*

The ferryman saw it too. "We'll steam ahead of him," he said, shouting over the racket of rain and wind, "pluck him up like a kitten."

The weather was not amenable to the rescue of flailing swimmers but the two men wordlessly agreed to it anyway, for biographies are nothing if not interstices between impetuous decisions. From the stern, the ferryman indicated the fire box amidships and Sequoia rose to shovel a spade of coal into its mouth. The pilot cranked the steam as far as it could go.

The sailor foundered in the chop, trying to stay afloat, the wind and current pushing him farther from grasp of his overturned boat. Sequoia guessed his age no older than thirteen, out sailing in a birthday or Christmas gift, too inexperienced to read the weather and too mule-headed to come in when told to. Some people shouted on the southern tip of a nearby island, pleading or encouraging the boy to swim, while another man fumbled to launch a dory kept turtled on the bank. The rain cut in scything blasts, so heavy the boy and skiff blurred into vague shapes drifting apart. Sequoia threw up an arm to shield his eyes.

The boy's head bobbed as the steam launch raced toward him. At the last moment they passed close, the boy gagging as every wave crested over his head, and the ferryman cut the launch hard in front of him, turning beam into the waves. The current pushed the boy against the launch's side as Sequoia jumped to the rail. Slippery as eels, the boy's arms slid through his grip but then Sequoia lunged at the boy's shirt and, grabbing the collar, dragged him over the rocking gunwale.

The boy collapsed, coughing and sputtering, and the ferryman reengaged the engine and turned toward the island. By mutual consent they considered the skiff lost, unless by some lucky roll of dice it wrecked on Horse Island or Outer, the last-chance plots of earth before open water.

"Can you breathe?"

The boy nodded.

"Good thing. This rain's so thick, we might need gills."

On almost every Thimble the dock was built into the rocks of its north shore to shelter it from the waves of Long Island Sound. As they beat against the wind toward Todeket's dock, the figures on the island waved as if the launch was unsure of the boy's provenance, and Sequoia wondered if they thought the ferryman intended to drop him at an orphanage in town. Sequoia waved back and pointed north.

They gesticulated even wilder, like castaways eager for rescue.

Sequoia just shrugged and they steamed on. The figures vanished behind a screen of pines. Todeket was a substantial Thimble, little more than an acre but heavily treed, so much so that a passerby could hardly tell what went on there.

A man waited at the dock. By his lumpy shape Sequoia recognized him as the one fooling with the overturned dory, now forgotten, and from his worn coat deduced he was a family manservant. He threw him a painter and the man pulled the steamboat to the boards, opposite a large sailboat. The boy took the man's hand and jumped onto the planks, followed by Sequoia, the two of them scrambling as if every falling grain in the glass was a lost hour of life. Sequoia turned for his bags but the ferryman was already throwing them into his arms. In return Sequoia tossed the line back onto the boat. The ferryman pushed off and turned toward the mainland without farewell or payment, disgusted he'd been coerced into taking passengers at all.

The manservant waved at Sequoia to follow. None of them spoke, the rain like the pounding of a thousand bill collectors on a thousand doors, and they ran stoop-backed down a path between pine branches and up the steps to an open kitchen door crowded with anxious faces.

Inside, a crush of people immediately surrounded the boy, either praising or scolding him while others fussed with towels or simply stared. Sequoia stood dripping and forgotten on the threshold, watching with some embarrassment as the family, every one of them a stranger, revealed themselves. The woman kneeling before the boy, hair wet and face self-possessed, holding his head between her hands, could only be the relieved mother; while the well-dressed man standing over him with grim expression and a stream of reprimands was assuredly the disciplinarian father. Almost hidden behind a cabinet stood a wide-eyed silent girl, a younger sister, and as Sequoia watched, the heat rose to her cheeks and she burst out crying, overwhelmed by the emotion around her. An older woman, a domestic, dried the boy's hair with a towel and peeled away his soaked outer layers. Less clear was the role of the handsome young woman who immediately comforted the crying girl; perhaps an aunt or cousin of theirs, vacationing at the house.

Sequoia felt as if he passed by the front window of a home set close to the street, only to glance inside to witness the occupants undressing. To give himself something to do, he turned and shut the back door, blocking the curtain of water that poured off the eaves.

The father turned from his lecturing to notice Sequoia. He reached into his pocket and jangled for coins.

"I suppose you're hanging around for your fare. How much is it?"

"There's no fare, sir," said Sequoia. To the father clearly all the world was a valet or doorman waiting with his palm out. "The boatman already departed. I'm a passenger, here at the invitation of my uncle, Preston Wescott."

The man's face didn't lighten an ounce. "Yes, I believe my father mentioned something about that. You mustn't let this episode inform your opinion of the family. My son is a fine sailor, as are all Wescotts, but he must learn to watch the weather. He can be foolish."

"Boys can be that—I was once one myself. A fine day until the clouds rolled in, and I suppose he was too busy enjoying his sailboat to notice."

"You were unable to throw a line around the boat, tow it to shore?"

"We didn't even make the attempt. Our plate was full with the blow."

"Pity a more able seaman didn't happen along instead," said the boy's father. "Well, I suppose the vessel is driftwood now—"

His sentence went unfinished. Sequoia's eyes focused on something behind the man while the bustle of the room siphoned into silence.

In the doorway to the interior of the house stood an old woman in a dressing gown. She leaned with one hand on the jamb, exhausted from her arrival, half of her hair pulled from its bun and floating around her head. The young woman crossed over to seize her free hand, as if afraid the lady might topple over. The old woman took several shuffling steps forward, her gaze briefly flickering on the boy before returning to their first regard.

"You," she said to Sequoia. "You saved my grandson's life. I witnessed the whole thing."

Sequoia glanced at the others, seeking some cue as

how to react to this phantom. The whole room, even the children, waited with a kind of awkward reverence, as if her presence was a visitation.

"You flatter me, ma'am," Sequoia said finally. "Most likely he could've swum to a nearby island. I'm told all the island children are strong swimmers." He very much doubted the truthfulness of his statement—but modesty usually made the best grease for the wheels of sociability.

"To you, small effort," said the woman, "and yet an invaluable favor to us. You cannot understand the gravity of it. For too long Death's black robe has hung over this family, and in saving Eli, you have swept the shadow from our doorstep."

She dictated this speech with grave and theatrical oration. Sequoia wondered if she was trained as an actress. The matriarch of the Wescott family, he knew, was famed in New York.

Her words visibly pained the boy's father. "Mother, please—"

"Be quiet, Andrew." The old woman didn't even glance at him. She walked closer to Sequoia. "What's your name, child?"

Something about her solemn manner made him state in full, as if he stood before a magistrate. "Sequoia Owen."

"Sequoia Owen. The son of my husband's sister. And the other man in the boat with you? What is his name?"

Again his gaze roved over the others for help. They simply waited for his answer.

"The pilot? I didn't catch his name, ma'am."

"I'm not speaking of the ferryman. I mean the *other* man. I clearly saw from the window there were three figures in the vessel. The ferryman sat at the tiller while the other stood beside you as you pulled Eli aboard."

Her eyes held his, and, gazing back, Sequoia searched for lunacy or senility. He shivered in his wet clothes.

"Ah," Sequoia said, shaking his head, "that's not possible. There was just the boatman and me."

For a heartbeat the entire room stood as a museum at midnight, the only sound the drumming of the rain on roof and pane.

"I see," she said with hesitant recognition. "Then it wasn't a man at all."

Andrew said low to the young woman, "Mattie." Not a request. A command.

"Ma'am," said Mattie, and suddenly Sequoia realized the unplaced young woman wasn't an aunt or a family member but rather a nurse, "let's return to the bedroom, please. Too much excitement." She took the old woman's arm and gently pulled her toward the staircase at the front of the house.

The woman allowed herself to be led a few steps before turning back toward Sequoia.

"Sequoia Owen," she said, "thank you for breaking the malaise over this family. The spirits are with us again. And apparently, also with you."

2

Experience instructed that locals in any port are often reluctant to spill their lore to out-of-towners but Sequoia knew that old salts grow more garrulous the later the clock strikes, especially as empty glasses accumulate on the bar top. So upon arriving in town the night before, he went searching for intelligence on the Wescotts. A lodging house located ten steps from the water's edge called the Indian Point House offered vacancy.

In the downtown saloon Sequoia casually mentioned his former career as a merchant mariner, and in so doing, established a certain fraternity with the regulars, aided by the discriminate funding of a few rounds.

What Sequoia learned about his hosts wouldn't have filled half a page in a ship's log. Beyond their summer house on Todeket Island, the Wescotts held few ties to the state, living most of the year in the city. The same biography could be spelled about many of the summer people, but generally the rest came by locomotive and horse car and availed themselves of the ferryboats so they were recognized and known by the townspeople. Yet the Wescotts were sailors themselves, voyaging from and to New York without bothering the ferrymen, so they largely remained strangers to the locals. The family employed a pair of servants, a married couple, who came to town once or twice a week in a dory to purchase groceries and necessities; and sometimes other members landed on shore—again, rowed by the manservant—to take day trips into New Haven. Other than that, all Sequoia learned from these natives was that Preston Wescott was a wealthy muckety-muck of unknown taxonomy and his wife was well known among the New York gentry.

But one of the tars in the saloon pulled at his clay pipe and, not knowing he chatted with the subject's own grandson, said he knew a story about the first Wescott to own Todeket Island. A fresh glass topped with suds appeared before him.

When the war started, Isaiah Wescott hurried to jot down his name with the US Navy. Nothing less than the navy would do for him. He was a sailor like all Wescotts and he'd be damned if he was stuck with a bunch of farmer boys in the army.

His eldest son, Preston, barely out of his teens, walked up to an enrollment tent and immediately enlisted as an ordinary seaman. Being a common sailor was out of the question for a man of Isaiah's pride and age, and because he brought no special talents or expertise to the table, the navy declined to offer him an officer's commission. Isaiah tried waving his purse around, but by then the navy frowned on men buying their way into the service and the rank wasn't for sale. The navy shut its door in his face.

The Marine Corps, however, wasn't as fussy, considering how a third of their officers defected to gray at the secession. An unhappy choice, but the marines were at least closer to the water than the army, so Isaiah purchased himself a lieutenancy and marched off to the bugle.

In November of the first year of the war, the navy captured Port Royal Sound and occupied Beaufort, the largest town south of Charleston, South Carolina. Charleston was too well defended to invade directly; and, in fact, the Union wouldn't take it until the conflict's final weeks. The strategy at the time was for the Federals to surround the city and then gradually squeeze their fist. Beaufort lay close to Charleston and served as their base.

The town sat upriver of the Sound, surrounded by an endless morass of swamps and inlets, and it was up to Wescott and his detachment to reconnoiter the bayous and clean up any Johnny Rebs who might be camped in the bush or locate any coves or creeks where a privateer might lay hidden.

Their expeditions moved in elliptical routes, looping out from Beaufort and back again every few days to report what they'd found. With most of the plantation owners off at war, escaped slaves streamed into the now-liberated town, and from these Wescott cobbled together rough maps of the land, dotted with buildings and places where they might hope to find fresh water and, by merit of common necessity, maybe the enemy too. Yet one area of his map remained terra incognita, about which none of the now-freedmen seemed to know. If they did, they only mentioned it in fearful tones. This empty space interested Wescott above all others, for nothing makes a sailor or marine more nervous than a fog bank.

So after several tours through the countryside, Wescott was able to convince his superiors the unknown area warranted an investigation, and, permission granted, he and his men set off.

The bayou was very dense, and once they abandoned their vessels, they found themselves hacking through a wilderness of vines and roots forsaken by everything except serpents and vermin of every crawling and flying species.

After nearly two days of this, the marines emerged from the trees to find a grand old plantation house squatting upon some high ground. At first they thought it was abandoned. Saplings had overtaken the former fields; the porch roof drooped half collapsed, with vines corkscrewed around its four Corinthian columns; and Spanish moss hung from the balcony over the front doors. A pair of eyebrow windows, both dark, peered down at them. But then an old woman strolled onto the porch waving an ancient flintlock, and inbetween profanities she demanded the Yankees take their asses back to Boston.

For a moment, the marines stood in awe of this absurdity. Then Isaiah Wescott marched up to the porch and grabbed the musket out of her hands while the old woman fumbled, the flint failing to light the wet powder in the barrel.

He turned to yell over his shoulder. "Sergeant!"

The man, whose name was Bauer, ran over. "Sir."

"Establish a perimeter and tell the men to set their tents in the yard," said Wescott. "We will be camping here tonight. Also, inform the cook to commandeer the kitchen and make use of any victuals he finds therein."

"Aye, sir," said Bauer.

The old woman shook with rage. "On my land? You have no right."

"I have every right," said Wescott. "And if your land and belongings are so precious to you, then your menfolk shouldn't have taken potshots at Fort Sumter."

"I have no menfolk. *You* men are nothing but thieves and bandits."

"No, ma'am, you're wrong. Thieves and bandits take what they want without compensation. We, however, are United States Marines, and when we leave my sergeant will be happy to give you a receipt for the items taken. I suggest you present it to Jefferson Davis for reimbursement." Wescott turned back to Bauer. "Sergeant."

"Yessir?"

He handed Bauer the flintlock. "Put this first on the list."

The marines searched the house and found no one else. The manse consisted of three connected build-

ings. The main house was Greek Revival, built of brick
with tall narrow windows, high ceilings, and nothing
less than four-piece moldings along the door and window frames. This was a more recent addition than the
kitchen in the back, a large single room little better than
a log cabin, likely dating from the first colonial settler
on the land. A sort of closed-in breezeway connected
the two, containing a formal dining room with several
rooms above.

And yet its grandeur was faded, for none of the
floors were flat, wallpaper hung peeled from the plaster, and in the upper chambers, stains of black mold
indicated a roof in disrepair. Exploring the house made
Wescott uneasy, for the stairs seemed ready to snap
under every footfall and in certain corners he spotted
droppings that suggested rats of abundant number.
The dust on the floorboards in some rooms indicated
no one had entered in months, and Wescott had the
impression the old woman lived mostly in the kitchen.
The house hadn't known other inhabitants for many
years.

"You are a family much reduced," said Wescott to
the old woman. She followed at his heels throughout
the house in grudging resignation to his presence,
like a conquered barbarian chief yielding to the new
Roman governor. Her family name was Desole, the
great-granddaughter of Huguenots.

"We are not reduced so much as attacked," said the
woman. "The Desole name carries on but the rest have

scattered. I'm the only one to remain here in the place where our family established itself on this continent."

"I can't imagine why any of your kin would flee your charming and agreeable nature."

She eyed him narrowly. "It wasn't me, Yankee. It was this house. None of them could stand to live here, and if they did, they spent their hours in quarrel and dispute."

Wescott snorted. "You describe many families, believe me. It has nothing to do with houses."

"This was worse. There were feuds. Duels," said the woman. "Murders."

Wescott shrugged. "I don't believe in ghost stories. Whatever strife and rancor you southern Judases experience, they are of your own creation."

"Our troubles began long before your aggression, Yankee," she said. "Abuse me all you wish. Kill me if you want. When I die, I ain't going anywhere." And with her hand she caressed the wallpaper.

"You plan to haunt your own house?" Wescott said lightly, humoring her. "A rather severe plan for avoiding Hell's Ninth Circle, I should think. The realm reserved for traitors."

"Think again. It is far worse."

"How can existence as a ghost be worse than an eternity in Hell?"

"Because," said the woman, "this house will soon be abandoned forever. And here, the only escape is through the door opened by a newcomer."

At the completion of his survey, Wescott selected the least appalling bedroom as his own. He opened the shutters to let in the late afternoon sun and shook the dust from the bed covers. Sleeping on a four-poster bed was a great improvement upon pitching a tent in a mosquito-plagued fen, and yet he felt a reluctance to stay in the house for long. Something about it strained Wescott's nerves. Not a single surface was level; not a single wall stood straight. Everything leaned or bowed. The stone foundation appeared solid enough, and yet he imagined the mud sucking the whole edifice downward, warping every perpendicular and kinking every plumb line. It was a house of jitters.

As he sat down to his morning breakfast in the dining room, Sergeant Bauer noted the dark bags under his lieutenant's eyes. "Trouble sleeping, sir?"

Wescott reached for his cup, filled with hot chicory coffee by a private. "I had the most horrible dream. As I lay in bed in the room upstairs, everything went very still and quiet. I opened my eyes and saw a man standing over me."

"You opened your eyes while awake or in the dream?"

"In the dream. But it was very real."

"What did he say?"

"The man? Nothing. Nothing at all. Just stood there, looking down at me. I tried to speak or get up but I found I couldn't move. I lay there utterly paralyzed. I could do nothing but regard him as he regarded me."

Bauer said, "And he did nothing?"

"No. I couldn't see him properly. Just a shadow really, standing there with a hunched back or rucksack, I couldn't tell. I just remember his attention, almost as if he judged me. Eventually the dream fell away but I slept very poorly after that."

Bauer was about to mention how his mother used to believe in a nocturnal witch who would press on men's chests while they slept, but at that moment a corporal burst in and, after apologizing, informed Wescott that scouts had discovered a rebel encampment nearby.

By the time they arrived, the camp had been hastily evacuated with the coals in the cooking fire still warm. They estimated a dozen men, rangers who'd been skirting around the edges of Beaumont sniping and making forays against the perimeter. Testing the Union troops, seeing what worked and what didn't.

As they studied the site, trying to accurately gauge how many bedrolls had laid on the ground, gunfire clapped in the woods to their right. Several of the troops sighted the retreating rebels and a running back and forth ensued as they gave chase. Or, more accurately, were led, for their pursuit drew them along a path into a swamp. Wescott suspected their quarry consisted of a few grays while the bulk hid among the trees and pools flanking them, ready to cut them down should they go any farther—an ambush. He ordered the men to fall back to the house.

They experienced no further incidents that day. Wescott was reluctant to depart as planned, for now he knew the rangers were close by, and he hoped they might be tempted to lay siege to the house in an open confrontation. It was a battle Wescott was confident they'd win, but though the men threw up impromptu barriers of brush and wood and kept a vigilant guard, no attack occurred.

Disappointed, Wescott concluded they must leave the house the following morning and continue their sweep through the countryside.

It was with some reluctance that Wescott entered his commandeered bedroom that night, and a grim foreboding filled him as he eyed the four-poster bed and its timeworn linens. Yet he undressed and laid himself down, to soon fall deeply asleep.

As before, he woke at some unknown midnight hour, aware of a pair of men standing over him, their faces cast in unperceivable shadow.

"Surrender, Lieutenant," said one. "While you slept like a lazy dog, we entered your camp and took your men hostage. You're the last one."

"No sense in fighting," said the other figure. "Come along quietly."

Initially Wescott did nothing but lie there, wondering at this visitation. But then in short order, he recalled two things. Firstly that, as a precaution, before climbing into bed he had taken with him his sidearm as a ward against the recurrence of phantasms. And secondly, unlike the previous evening, his limbs were not paralyzed.

He drew and fired, and one of the shadows, taken by the suddenness of it, dropped to the floorboards. The other bolted for the window, and in the tumult set off by the gunshot, was captured after leaping into the midst of the marines in the yard. Talk of the Union men having surrendered was a ruse to coerce Wescott himself into yielding.

Upon interrogation of the two men—the one he'd shot through the lung would, within hours, drown in his own blood—Wescott learned the running gunfight of the previous morning had been orchestrated as a distraction, allowing for the two rangers to infiltrate the unguarded house and wait until nightfall, when they intended to kidnap the commanding Union officer to use in a future prisoner exchange.

Further pressed, they explained they'd hidden in the basement beneath the more recent portion of the house, which having been already searched the first day, went unsearched the second. Once most of the marines, save the perimeter guards, had drifted off to sleep, the rangers crept from their hidey-hole and went upstairs to capture Wescott. Alas for them, his prior nightmare had thwarted them.

It was beyond reason to think the old crone knew nothing about the two men's presence in her home,

and when asked if she'd personally hidden them in the
basement, she couldn't keep from beaming. Wescott
ordered the men to loot the house, taking anything of
value or, frankly, anything that caught their fancies. The
woman stopped smiling after that. Her humor further
vanished when Wescott told the men to light brands
and throw them through the doors and windows.

As smoke rolled from the apertures, the widow
Desole cursed and cursed them a thousand times,
reserving most of those curses for Isaiah Wescott.
Ransacking done, the marines began their march into
the woods with their laden packs and sole surviving
prisoner. But as Wescott bid adieu and stepped off the
porch, Desole reached to the ground and pulled up a
rock to hurl at Wescott, striking him in the head and
knocking him out cold.

Without thinking, Bauer swung his rifle toward her
and shot her dead. The marines buried her where she
fell, without marker or headstone, and that was the last
any of them saw of the Desole plantation.

So simple a wound and yet Wescott's recuperation
was long and difficult. His senses addled, simple tasks
proved challenging. He eventually recovered, but his
superiors moved him into an administrative role before
finally mustering him out.

Before the war Isaiah Wescott had started a business
in New York and summered in Connecticut, where he
came to love the Thimble Islands. Some of the outer

islands were, at that time, still available, and he bought Todeket—named after *Totoket*, the Mattabesec Indian name for the mainland town—cheap because of its distance and unimproved state.

Yet those who knew him said Wescott changed after the war, and they muttered how his former calm demeanor melted into hot tempers and even violent rages. They noted how the servants turned over mighty quickly, except for a few trusted loyalists. They speculated such strangeness passed into the home he built on the island.

At this point the old shellbacks at the saloon fell to discoursing upon the nature of Wescott's two nights spent at the Lowcountry plantation. If the visitors of the second evening turned out to be Confederate rangers, then who stood over Wescott's bed on the *first* night? They could hardly be the same, for the rebels admitted they'd stolen into the house that very morning. Suffice to say the initial shadow was a figment—but only because of it was Wescott preserved from the second.

As an epilogue, the storyteller mentioned the time Sergeant Bauer, passing through Connecticut on his way home after attending Grant's funeral in New York, visited Todeket Island to reunite with his former commanding officer. By that time Wescott lay several years in the grave. Upon returning to the mainland, Bauer stopped in at the Stony Creek saloon—for it was from him that the locals learned the preceding tale.

It was Bauer's opinion that something about the plantation house spoke to Wescott, something that made him believe it would defend and sustain him. He couldn't imagine any other reason why the home Isaiah Wescott built on Todeket Island was the spitting replica of the old woman's house they'd found in the swamp.

3

The old cook led Sequoia to a spartan room on the third floor. It contained a bed, a chair, a chipped bureau, and a ceiling that brushed his scalp. Sequoia noted it lay near the rooms inhabited by her and her husband, as well as that of Mrs. Wescott's nurse—he was being lodged with the servants.

"Surely I might have a bedroom on the floor below? I believe I saw some empty chambers."

"Those are reserved for the party guests tonight," said the woman. "Sometimes the guests of Mr. and Mrs. Wescott prefer to stay over."

"Ah—too drunk to make it home."

She ignored him. "Bring your wet things downstairs and I'll hang them by the stove." And she left with her mouth drawn tight.

In some annoyance Sequoia tossed his carpetbag onto the bed. His other luggage—the small wooden case with a leather strap for a handle—he carefully set on the bureau. He changed into dry clothes, and as instructed, returned to the kitchen with his sodden laundry.

The storm thrashed and howled outside, the gusts throwing water against the windows like handfuls of pebbles. Sequoia sat at the kitchen table sipping a cup of coffee the cook wordlessly offered him. He could tell she was the type to forever hold his joke upstairs as a grievance. A bad habit, he knew, to sometimes say out loud the contents of his mind, a habit learned from years at sea where one clipped his words in the presence of superiors but spoke frankly to those beneath.

Everyone had vanished somewhere within the house, presumably to look after little Eli following his experience, or Mrs. Wescott after hers, so he sat watching the storm through the glass while the cook silently chopped and sliced, no doubt wishing every potato she cut into was Sequoia's throat.

"Is my uncle Preston in the house?" he asked her.

"Aye," she said without glancing up from her knife. "He'll see you when he's ready. Not before."

He almost laughed at her impertinence. "What put you in such a bad mood? The weather?"

"I don't answer incivility."

"I'm just wondering if you're like this to all the guests."

She didn't respond immediately. "If you must know," she said, "it's a bad sign, Mrs. Wescott seeing what she saw. No good will come of it."

"Seeing what? A third man in the boat?"

"Aye." She had a faint accent, unplaceable but not necessarily foreign. "Seeing *him* always means a death's coming."

"Who's him?"

"Not my place to say. I've never seen him and I hope never to."

"But who do you mean? A ghost?"

The word was like camphor to a clothes moth. The old cook immediately turned her back toward him to fiddle with the stove. He was for all intents and purposes alone in the kitchen.

No choice, then, but to drink hot coffee and wait patiently, which suited Sequoia fine after his soaking.

The trees closely crowded the house. The culling of storms probably kept the pitch pines of the islands, scraggly and tenacious in their offshore banishment, from growing too tall. Studying them, Sequoia questioned if anyone on either of the upper floors of the house had a clear view of the water. His aunt said she'd seen the steam launch from her window.

A sound gradually rose over the noise of wind and rain outside. Like the rumble of an approaching locomotive, it began as a vague vibration, growing louder the longer he listened, as indiscernible syllables germinated into words and phrases and, eventually, wholly legible sentences.

Floating toward him from some other room, two incorporeal voices screamed at one another. Easy enough to distinguish, one male, one female, the pattern fluctuated as each voice, having articulated its point, would allow the other to speak in turn, back and forth like the ball in a tennis match, until the intonation and speed of both speakers increased and they ran over each other.

As no proper names were used but only pronouns, the gist of the dispute wasn't immediately clear, and only after awkward eavesdropping did he surmise it regarded the accident of which Sequoia himself had been the solution. The lady blamed the man for pushing *him* too hard and too far, while her opponent blamed *his* inexperience on her coddling and bad mothering.

Finally the cacophony lulled, followed by some loud thumps as if something fallen or slammed, and then silence. A few moments later, the manservant reappeared in the kitchen.

"Hello again," Sequoia said to the man.

"He can't hear you," said the cook, breaking her silence. "He's as deaf as a bucket."

"A good trait to have hereabouts."

"Keeping a respectful tongue is a better one," said the cook.

The man pointed at his chest. "Burke," he said, his voice deep from disuse. He pointed to the woman and contorted his mouth, his words exaggerated. "Wife."

"*Mrs. Burke*, if you please."

Introductions established, Burke waved at Sequoia to follow.

He led Sequoia down a corridor into the front of the house and deposited him alone in an uninhabited study, closing the pocket doors behind him. Sequoia's hands missed the warm cup and he rubbed them together, taking in the chamber, the bookshelves, the naval cutlass on the heavy desk, the decanter of whis-

key and glasses upon the sideboard. Directly he swept
for the bookshelf covering the wall beside the desk.
Like most formal libraries, the volumes were mostly
for show, removed from their places only when the
room was dusted. Elsewhere in the house—probably
on the second floor, hidden from guests—would be a
stash of the books the Wescotts actually read, rows of
novels and romances and popular nonfiction. But these
books with their stiff spines and raised bands and gold
ink were like sphinxes arranged along a temple avenue,
meant to impress the visitor as he swept past them, to
awe the petitioner before his audience with Pharaoh.

His eyes glazed as they ran over the titles. Instinctively he dismissed the texts on law and natural phi-
losophy, slowing only when he arrived at the histories:
Gibbon, Tacitus, Thucydides, Xenophon. These he
scrutinized more carefully, noting which he'd read,
which he hadn't, which he'd read but forgotten, and
which he should read again.

As he paced along the row, a single volume stood
out. He pulled it from the shelf, examining the wear on
its head and foot bands, and it fell open with none of
the arthritis of an unread book. The frontispiece read:
A General History of the Pyrates, Volume Two.

A round tab of paper stood raised from the text
block. A bookmark. He flipped open to it, sandwiched
between the first pages of the final chapter.

The bookmark was a figure cut roughly from white

paper. Sequoia picked it up, and it fell open accordi-on-like—a series of paper dolls, connected at the hands and feet. There were no features or faces, only names written in small letters across their torsos. The last one—or the first one, the one that lay on top—was titled *Jacob*.

The pocket door slid open behind him and Sequoia slammed shut the book, crushing the paper dolls within.

"I see I'm not the only one curious about the story of William Kidd," said Preston Wescott.

Sequoia pushed the book back onto the shelf and turned to greet his uncle. He was tall and dressed a bit formally for the heat, his thick white muttonchops suggesting a tight-fisted conservatism that lent itself to finance, razor, and strop.

For a moment Sequoia hesitated, reconciling the man before him with the memory of the man from the funeral; and also with the man from the St. Nicholas. Then too there was another man, the one Sequoia knew from the newspaper articles he'd clipped and saved after the funeral. One described a lawsuit filed by a former friend and business partner of his uncle, who described Preston Wescott with pejoratives such as *ruthless* and *vindictive*. The second story was darker, noting how a well-known industry opponent had been dredged up with his lungs full of the Harlem River; it accused the Wescott name of nothing, only mentioning a long feud between the dead man and Preston Wescott.

A row of paper dolls stood before Sequoia, and of all of them he wondered which was the truth.

The older man's eyes ranged over Sequoia's clean-shaven face. "It's good to see you again, my boy," said Preston as they shook.

"You too, sir."

"Do you know much about Kidd's career?"

Sequoia shrugged. "Not particularly. Only the stories that he buried his treasure on every island along the Connecticut coast. Charles Island, Fishers Island. Someplace here in the Thimbles is supposed to be another. He must've been a squirrel in autumn, burying so many pieces-of-eight like acorns."

"I've heard that too. Old Man Brien used to advertise in the newspapers about a chunk of stone with the letters 'W.K.' carved into it near his hotel on High Island. He led tours to it, marveling as if it was Plymouth Rock."

Sequoia had yet to properly meet the family and already he liked the father much better than the son. "It's the same with everything, I suppose. Any inn or saloon with more than three generations of mice in its cellar will proclaim Washington slept there. People enjoy history, especially when it happened nearby. It makes them feel part of an experience grander than themselves."

Preston regarded him with fresh appraisal. "I'm astonished to hear you say so."

"Because I'm a sailor and a boatsman? You expected a simpler imagination."

Preston cleared his throat, evidently embarrassed. "Well, I suppose so, yes."

Sequoia nodded toward the history books. "Most of my education took place on merchant ships, crisscrossing the Atlantic. It's funny. I can look at a book and tell you where we were bound when I read it. I read Caesar's *Commentaries on the Gallic War* on the way to Nantes and the *Anabasis* on a return from Falmouth. Yet for my own life I couldn't tell you the month or even the year of the voyage."

"Memory *is* strange," said Preston. His furry brows knitted together. "It's most eclectic, and whether one recalls the good or dwells upon the evil is more a factor of constitution than anything else. Events are rarely remembered without prejudice. We edit and excise, pasting them into our own invisible histories, which we then reread continuously. And yet those books rarely agree with the volumes scribed by those who shared the same events with us. Wouldn't you agree?"

"I confess I've never thought about it. But what you say makes sense."

Preston nodded, and walked around to sit at his desk, indicating Sequoia should take a seat across from him. "The stories about Kidd's treasure were a particular obsession of my fa— well, I should say *your* grandfather. He purchased Todeket Island in part because some of the legends pointed to it as the resting place of the trove."

"Did he find it?"

"Not so much as a doubloon," said Preston. "Yet another of his eccentricities." His tone suggested embarrassment.

At this reference to money, Sequoia sat a little straighter, his eyes brighter.

"Anyway," said Preston, "I'm glad you're here and you have my sincerest thanks, Sequoia, for saving Eli. But I must doubly thank you for another service you performed, of which you are no doubt unaware. Your actions inadvertently rewrote a story my wife has been telling herself, for the better."

"I take it the lady I met earlier in the kitchen is my aunt. She was very gracious."

"She is never anything but, to anyone. That's not the greatest surprise. Allow me to explain what to you must seem opaque. Not long ago, our oldest son died unexpectedly. The elder brother to Andrew, whom you've already met. It devastated my wife."

"Jacob?"

"Yes."

"Was he a navy man like you? I hope he wasn't a casualty of this stupid war."

At the mention of the current conflict, a twitch of irritation passed over his uncle's face. "It was an accident," said Wescott, his words clipped. For the first time, a certain hostility radiated from the man. "Regardless, my wife lost all interest in socializing or attending the theater, or even leaving the house. She was so inconsolable she wouldn't even eat or drink.

After some difficulty, we brought her to the island last summer, as we always do, in the belief these salubrious shores would revitalize her. They didn't, and at the end of the season she refused to depart. She's been on the island ever since."

"I'm surprised she over-wintered here." Even as a newcomer to the Thimbles, Sequoia realized wintering on the islands must be unusual, even difficult. The ferrymen themselves probably didn't stick around so there would be no launch service. The weather prevented easy travel between the mainland, and summer houses weren't designed for the cold. Just then he recalled seeing a large stack of firewood outside as he stood at the kitchen door, orange needles covering the logs like a horse blanket.

"She stayed, along with the servants and her nurse. I visited when I was able but my business keeps me in New York most weeks. I tell you this so that you may comprehend the distress under which my family has labored. You cannot conceive what it has been like for me to return to this house yesterday to find my wife still gripped by melancholy after so many long months, only to discover her ebullient and restored within the last hour."

"You mean since I retrieved your grandson?"

"Yes. She is upstairs dressing as we speak, something she hasn't done since—well, I can't remember when."

"I take no credit for that."

"You may not take it but I'll dispense it all the same.

She's weakened by her privation, and yet there's a light in her eyes and an excitement in her voice that's been absent for too long. Which brings me to my proposition." He regarded me. "Are you familiar with the Knickerbocker Yacht Club?"

"No, sir."

"They're a sailing club in New York. The Wescotts are among the founding families. Every year, at the beginning of August, the club sails east into the Sound and drops anchor in the Thimbles for two weeks. There are parties and regattas. Here at the house we traditionally host a celebration for a few members on the first Saturday of the month."

"I'm very flattered to be included."

"It's a small affair. But you see, this year Mrs. Wescott declined to attend—she said she wouldn't dress or come downstairs. That is, until just now."

"She's that transformed?"

"Yes. Moreover, she wishes to hold a séance tonight after dinner. She hasn't held one since," he said, his throat catching, "since our son's passing. And she very much wants you to take part tonight."

Sequoia shook his head. "I'm afraid I don't understand."

Preston leaned forward and folded his hands upon the desk. "What do you know about your aunt?"

"Only that she is famous in New York. Very famous."

This seemed to gratify Preston. "My wife *is* famous. She's a well-respected spiritualist in the city. There was a waiting list for her weekly séances. Did you know the mayor's wife once attended?"

"News of New York society rarely reaches Virginia."

"She did. She leapt up babbling in French when the spirit of Marie Antoinette possessed her." Preston nodded in reminiscence, relishing the memory of so important a personage, either mayoral spouse or last queen of France, sitting in his parlor. "What your aunt saw today has shaken her, and what happens *tonight* could make the difference."

Throughout this last colloquy, excitement slowly rose inside Sequoia's chest. "You may not believe this," he said, "but up in my guest room I have something that may interest you greatly."

"Is that so?"

"If you'll allow me, I'll go fetch it."

Preston, clearly mystified, nodded, and within the space of two minutes Sequoia returned with the case. He placed it on the desktop, undid a pair of latches, opened the lid, and from within produced a rectangular wooden box, stained and handsomely made, which he set before his uncle. In its face were four brass reels on which words had been painstakingly engraved, while on the side was a button or switch not unlike the latch of an old door. From the same case, Sequoia produced a key, which he inserted in the back of the box and wound until it stopped. "I call it the Mechanical Oracle," he said. "It's a prototype which I hope to mass produce."

"A Mechanical Oracle?" Preston leaned forward to examine it. "I don't understand."

"It's very simple. Ask a question of the Oracle, and when you want an answer, simply press the button on the side."

"You mean it replies?"

"In a sense. Go ahead and ask it a question."

"Out loud?"

"Of course. That way both of us knows what was asked."

Preston studied it a minute more, and then, perhaps imagining it was some sort of telephone, lowered his mouth toward the box and said, "What are we having for supper?" He pressed the button.

Immediately the four reels spun very fast with a clicking sound. Suddenly, one, then the rest, stopped, revealing four sets of words which together made a pair of brief sentences.

"What does it say?"

"*The forecast suggests trouble*," Preston read. "*Your future is in doubt.*" He looked at Sequoia and burst out laughing. "It certainly has Mrs. Burke's number. One cross word directed at her and we'll both be supping on cold chicken."

"Ask again. But this time, ask it something that concerns you. A more personal question."

"Yes, yes. I see." Preston thought a moment. Then a question occurred to him and he leaned toward the machine again. "Will tonight be a success?" He pressed the button.

Again the reels spun, then halted. "*The answer will be revealed soon. Your fate is insufficient.* 'Your fate is insufficient'—that doesn't make much sense."

"I admit the specific phrases need some adjustment."

Preston nodded up and down. "Still. A simple clockwork inside I presume, powered with springs?"

"Exactly," said Sequoia. "I had the idea years ago while in France. Fortune tellers and cartomancers are very common in Brest and Le Havre, especially by the docks. They use common decks of playing cards. They tell the person's fortune by laying out a certain number of cards and then interpreting them. It occurred to me a machine could do much the same—say, four reels, one for each suit, and each reel featuring eight cards on them. But then I realized that the selection of playing cards would be meaningless for most without the reader to interpret them, so instead of cards I engraved actual replies on the reels."

"Which produces a random fortune. Wonderful."

"This is just a prototype, you understand. There are four phrases on each dial, so there's only sixteen possible messages for each of the two lines. I imagine something much more sophisticated for the final version, with five, six, or even eight reels. My ultimate vision is for the machine to produce whole quatrains like Nostradamus—you know, those kinds of cryptic messages that seem so profound but could mean anything."

"Gives the guests something to chatter about."

"I think the madness for spiritualism would lend itself to sales."

"I quite agree," said Preston. "Everyone would want one in their house, like a phonograph." Uncle Preston looked at Sequoia and said, "I see you are already something of a spiritualist like your aunt. You'll be a great help at the séance."

"I hardly know the first thing about spiritualism or séances. This is just a notion of mine meant to appeal *to* spiritualists."

Preston waved his hand. "I don't expect you to know anything. It's very simple. The important thing is that your aunt feels you are accompanied by a helpful spirit, the first she's perceived since the accident. Your cooperation is crucial. And, I might add, to her recovery."

"How so?"

"Well, because of some rather silly stories and legends about this house. My wife will undoubtedly ask specific questions of the spirit, and I can guess beforehand what some of those questions may be. It's vital that the replies—which you will be expected to give—soothe her peace of mind. Sort of like your machine. They must relieve the anxieties and doubts she has about our son's death."

"You want me to—what? Pretend I am possessed by a spirit and provide certain answers."

"You fathom the situation to its depths." Preston eyed him carefully. "You know, this device of yours—this Mechanical Oracle—has great potential. I mean it, Sequoia. Perhaps if you could see fit to help our family, I would be willing to invest in your idea—to give you the money you need to expand it, hire some craftsmen to produce more machines, and then get them into stores. An Oracle in every home. What do you say?"

The elasticity of the clock is a phenomenon commonly reflected upon, particularly by those in moments of great importance. The space between ticks expands, and yet the speed at which everything moves remains constant: if anything, the heart beats quicker and the beads of the mind's abacus fly back and forth along their strings. Such was Sequoia's experience sitting in the chair, staring at Preston Wescott.

"I can see the séance, done properly, would help my aunt tremendously," Sequoia said at last. "So of course you can expect my full assistance."

"Excellent!" They stood and shook hands.

The audience complete, Preston walked Sequoia to the pocket doors and told him to make himself at home. He also explained it was customary for the gentlemen to congregate in his office before dinner for a drink.

"I've yet to compliment you on your beautiful house," said Sequoia. "I saw a number of the island cottages on the ferry out and this is by far the grandest."

"Yes," said Preston. "Everyone agrees my father spent far too much money on it. More space than necessary for a summer house, really. But something about its architecture convinced him it was unique, something that put him closer to God. Your grandfather had a number of, shall we say, unusual ideas. He collected feathers, for example, that he found around the island. Kept a box full of them. Claimed they came from the wings of angels." He tapped his right temple. "But they were just gull feathers."

"I understand he sustained an injury during the war. That he was struck by a stone and suffered a concussion. Perhaps that explains his idiosyncrasies."

"A stone?" Preston shook his head. "Oh no, my dear boy. He was shot through the skull with a bullet. Blew out part of his brain and yet miraculously he lived. A good man, my father, but God help him, he was insane."

Then his uncle beamed and clapped Sequoia on the back. "I look forward to tonight. If I cannot bring my wife back to New York, then I shall bring New York to *her*."

4

Before leaving him, his uncle led Sequoia down a zigzag hallway to the parlor at the front of the house where he presented him with a thick album. He then mentioned some business and promised to see Sequoia again before supper.

Flipping through, it occurred to Sequoia the volume was a fixture of the parlor itself, a commonplace book that functioned as a history of Todeket Island and the summer house. At least a dozen different hands were evident in its pages, and he imagined its contents were a project puttered at during long summer afternoons when the heat made other activities uncomfortable. There was a long list of the dates on which the house was opened up in the spring and when it was closed in late September, along with the weather conditions on those days, as well as a register of important events and holidays. There were few, if any, allusions to Christmases and Easters but great emphasis on Independence Days and picnics and sailing regattas.

Pasted among its heavy pages lay an old daguerreotype. It was a yellowed portrait of a family: the father and husband, seated and staring off to the viewer's left, his gaze vacant and yet his expression almost pained in its frowning consternation; behind him, a wife resigned to the ponderous burdens levied upon her; and to either side, a pair of stone-faced children, the sister older than the brother.

Sequoia wasn't entirely sure he'd ever met his grandparents. He possessed no memories whatsoever of his grandmother, and with secondhand facts about Isaiah Wescott so mixed up like cake batter in his head he couldn't say firmly if he'd ever known him either. There was no question of the Wescotts visiting the Owens in Virginia. Had his mother taken him to meet them on some neutral ground, as she had with Preston that day in New York at the St. Nicholas Hotel? And yet looking around at the parlor furniture and patterned wallpaper, all of it original to the house, a faint remembrance pulled at Sequoia. Like a pair of stereoscope images, each seen through a separate lens, the parlor he saw now and another dredged from the channel of his mind merged together into a strange familiarity. Connecticut born, he had no recollection of it. Had he been to that house on Todeket as a young child? As an infant?

Sequoia continued to turn the pages, crabbed with faded ink and newspaper clippings, only now with an emotion of lessening indifference. The Owens were so few they could fit around a card table: his father's parents both died young; and his aunts and uncles consisted of old maids and Western adventurers, his kinship with them no deeper than the affection felt for a neighbor's dog. But as he sat with the Wescott album in his lap, a warmth rose inside Sequoia, a happiness at a reunification he didn't know he'd missed. It summarized all that had been denied him by his father's severance to his mother's family. The happy summers, the Julys and Augusts of swimming and boating and climbing trees or jumping off rocks with blood-relations of various distinctions, the petty dramas and gossips of a family—all of it lost. Yet instead of anger or resentment over that erasure, inside Sequoia swelled a tenderness toward everything Wescott, an endearment to the family. He felt no resentment toward the injury, only a joy upon rediscovering health once the splints and plaster were sawed away.

A page listed deaths on the island.

9 Jul. 1868. Jer. Wescott. Drowned.
6 June 1872. Pearl Wescott. Drowned.
August 23, 1874. Benj. Hayward. Drowned.
Aug. 9, 1883. Gretch. Phelps Wescott. Drowned.
May 25, 1884. Esthr. Watkins. Fall.
July 26, 1885. Isaiah Wescott. Infirmity.
Sep 4, 1887. Silas Burbidge. Drowned.
3/25/90. L. Burke. Influenza.
8/9/97. J. Wescott. Accident.

He turned the page. It was headlined, in bold block letters overwritten several times for emphasis, *The Todeket Ghost.*

I was walking from the house through the trees to the south shore. Someone was walking ahead of me but when I called to them they wouldn't answer. When I reached the shore no one was there. (July 9 1868).

For the following two pages, the number of hands multiplied greatly, including some clearly belonging to children.

June 1872. In the bedroom I stay in there was a black pool at the end of the bed. As when there is a break in the clouds on an overcast day and the sun shines through but instead of a ray of light it was darkness.

17 July, 1873. There was a woman in the parlor standing by the window. She was dressed in a gray frock. When I asked her business she turned to face me but before I could make out her features she vanished.

Some were very brief.

August 21st, 1874. Shadow in the kitchen corner moved away when I entered.

23rd August, 1874. A woman stood observing from the shore as a group of rescuers tried but failed to save my brother who'd slipped below the surface. I don't know who the woman was.

Another was recorded by dictation.

May 29, 1875. Jonathan Wescott (age 4) insists he spoke to a young man in the yard. He says the other children saw and spoke to him as well but none of them say they did. Asked to describe the man, the description fitted that of Benjamin. But he had been leafing through the album the evening before.

A final deponent with some artistic skill included a charcoal sketch of her encounter, captioned thusly:

A man stepped out of the doorway to Lulu's room and

crossed the upstairs hallway in front of me to vanish through the wall to my left. His stride was firm and purposeful. July 2, 1875.

A moody tableau of blacks upon grays showed the silhouetted profile of a dark figure peering directly at the reader from behind a corner on the second-floor landing.

Footsteps shuffled. Sequoia looked up to see Andrew Wescott enter the parlor. He walked hunched forward, his arm wrapped across his face as if blinded, and collapsed into a chair. In his other hand he clutched a black-bound book. His body shook briefly and he let out a low groan.

Sequoia opened his mouth to ask what was the matter when the young woman from the kitchen also appeared, making a straight line for Andrew. She carried with her a small leather ditty bag.

"Hurry," said Andrew.

The nurse took Andrew's limp arm and rolled up his shirt sleeve. Then, from the unbuttoned kit, she withdrew a silk band which she tied around his bicep. A syringe and vial were produced, the syringe filled. Andrew grit his teeth while the long process of filling and examination occurred, his muscles pinched tight with pain. Finally she tapped the bulging vein, injected the syringe, and pushed the plunger.

As she undid her construction—a swab of cotton pressed against the injection site, the syringe and vial returned to their kit, the tourniquet removed—Andrew's arm fell off his face and his expression visibly relaxed.

It was as if a locomotive, having arrived at its terminal, was emptied of its passengers, every one of them irritable from the long journey and anxious to reach their destinations. The eyelids loosened, the wrinkles on his forehead smoothed like water beneath a dying wind, and his jaw slackened until the mouth opened. His head rolled slightly to the side, and Andrew drifted, if not to sleep, then into some twilight state neighboring it.

From the looks and glances she flashed Sequoia it was clear the nurse was aware of his presence in the room. She buttoned up her kit, took one last measure of Andrew's pulse, gently set his arm down into his lap, and then walked over to sit close beside Sequoia. They hadn't been properly introduced before, she said in a tone just above a whisper. Her name was Mattie Fuller.

"Initially I was hired by his wife—the younger Mrs. Wescott—to look after her mother-in-law. But it soon became clear that the family suffers from a variety of conditions."

"And what is Andrew's?"

"Intemperance." For a long moment she observed Andrew to confirm he was asleep. "We are engaged in a treatment in which we stretch the length of time between waking and his first drink of the day. Obviously I can only treat him when he's here on the island as his mother is my primary concern. However, we've made substantial progress—from less than four hours to eight and three-quarters."

"I assume you injected him with morphine."

Mattie shrugged. "The injection was the Keeley Cure." Sequoia had heard of it: a doctor set up a clinic in Illinois and drunkards stormed its doors, eager converts to Dr. Keeley's claims that he could inoculate their cravings away with a mysterious concoction. Regardless of whether Keeley discharged saloon keepers from their professions, his cure certainly increased Keeley's net worth.

"You're somehow certified or connected with the Keeley Institute?"

"Not at all. Anyone can order the cure through the post. You're supposed to drink it, but I convinced Andrew the result is better if injected instead. Part of the effect, I think, lies in the ritual. Whatever else is in it, you're right—I suspect it contains a good dose of morphine. When he wakes, he'll be calm for another hour or so, and then he'll drink until his next dose, or until he goes to bed."

Mattie's nose inclined over the top of the commonplace to see the page Sequoia was on. The hairs on his arms stood electrified, very aware of her closeness. She smelled of oranges and cloves. "The Todeket Ghost," she said. "I've never seen it but Geneve has—that's why she wants you at the séance tonight. She thinks the ghost likes you."

The situation crystallized in his head, like frost expanding across a cold windowpane. The boy's misadventure with the overturned sailboat, the sighting of an unknown figure in the boat beside him, both coinciding with Sequoia's arrival on the island. It fit with the legend.

"There's quite a long list of drownings recorded here," said Sequoia. "I'm glad to have helped prevent another."

"Too may drownings for coincidence."

Sequoia frowned. "The least experienced swimmers are often those who spend the most time around water. They become victims of their own comfort with the danger. I can imagine how easy it is to dive off the rocks of the island, only to be dragged down by some deep current, or to cramp in the cold water and drop like a stone to the bottom."

"If you read closely, you'll see the witnesses of the ghost fall into two parties," said Mattie. "Those in which the ghost was witnessed but misfortune was averted, and those who saw it accompanied by fatal tragedy."

"You're very familiar with the stories," Sequoia said.

"I've had long months to browse the album. Since last summer."

He searched her face for fatigue or an impatience to escape but didn't find as much of the emotion as expected.

"I was hired precisely for that reason," Mattie said. "Not only as a nurse but as Geneve's companion. When it came time to shut down the house for the season, she refused. At the very least the family is understanding. I have one free day a week, even if I am sometimes prevented from going into town by the weather. I don't mind the isolation—if anything, I feel like I've discovered much about myself here on the island. Still, I'm not sure it worked out the way it was intended. Familiarity breeds contempt."

"You dislike my aunt."

"Rather the opposite. Mr. Wescott was supposed to visit every weekend over the winter, but that didn't always occur. Same with Andrew and Lisette. Very often it was just me and Geneve, and the Burkes, of course. But Mr. Burke is deaf and Mrs. Burke isn't an endearing conversationalist. Geneve grew to mistrust me. I came to epitomize all the misgivings she has about the rest of her family. Especially in regard to Jacob's death."

"What were the circumstances, exactly?"

"He shot himself in the head," said Mattie. Her tone was clinical. "He was distressed over a love affair. His parents made him break it off."

"Awful."

"Yes. I wasn't here at the time, of course. None of them talk about it so everything I've learned has been slivers and fragments." She looked toward the doorway. "Speaking of which, I should check on Geneve. She wants to see you."

She paused to lock her eyes upon him. "You must understand something, Mr. Owen. Geneve is very sick.

Delusional, even. Many of her beliefs are harmless—most, I would say. But those beliefs she has regarding her son are very destructive, both for her and those who love her. You mustn't support those beliefs or give her any hope there's truth to them."

Sequoia said, "I'm not sure what you're asking of me."

"Just simply watch what you say and to think twice before you answer her." And with that, she stood and swept from the room.

As she passed, Andrew jerked awake, roused by the swishing of her skirts. He glanced in the direction from where she came and for the first time noticed Sequoia. For a moment he stared with clear wonderment questioning how long he'd been there, then leaned back into his seat and rubbed his eyes.

"Look at you, sitting there all cozy with the commonplace," Andrew said. "As if you lived here."

"I was just reading about the family legend. Your island is haunted."

Andrew frowned. "That stupid ghost. People jumping at shadows." He relaxed his head against the top rail of the chair and faced the ceiling with shut eyes. "My brother said he saw it once, as a child. It's one thing to play a children's game, another for adults to go along with it. I asked him about it years later when he should've known better, and he insisted he'd really seen it. He had a whole theory about it, mixed up with our grandfather's beliefs. Preposterous."

He rubbed his eyes, then began thumbing through the pages of the black book in his lap.

"I don't believe in ghosts either," said Sequoia. "But when several people say they saw something I tend to think they did, even if they misunderstand what they saw."

"It's fortunate that you don't work in business because you'd be very bad at it. When someone tells you something that's wrong, sorting it is always a waste of time. They're just wrong."

"You work in business?"

"Yes."

"What kind of business?"

"I work with my father."

"Doing what?"

"You mean you don't know? You really are a very *distant* relation."

"I still don't understand what you do for a living."

Andrew's head revolved toward Sequoia. "My father owns a large and rather well-known securities brokerage. I work for my father."

"So you're a broker. I feel like we went around Cape Horn to arrive at that answer."

"Ah yes. You're a merchant marine, so you've actually been around the Horn." He returned his attention to his book. "Do you know much about investing?"

"No," said Sequoia with more truth than he would've liked. "I've always allowed others to manage my funds."

"Do you use a broker? Which one?"

"A company called Midgley and Groves."

"I know them," said Andrew.

"And what is your opinion of their reputation?"

Andrew said without tone, "They're capable."

"That hasn't been my experience."

Andrew said nothing. Instead he held his book toward him, holding it open by the top so Sequoia could see the pages. It was a notebook, the creamy paper covered with figures and formulas and arithmetic drawn in various colored pencils. "Midgley and Groves do not have a *system*. I do. That's why our firm is so successful."

"Because of a system."

Andrew clapped the book shut. "Of course. A system. Most people consider the market a game of chance, no different than a round of faro in a saloon. It is not. The market is causal, one event rising from another. But—it is because the majority *believes* their fallacy that I succeed. By playing upon their beliefs, I have developed a foolproof system of investing."

"Using your father's capital, I'm sure."

"No. My system is all my own. I consider myself a self-made man."

Sequoia, who paged idly through the commonplace while they spoke, closed the album and set it on the windowsill. Whatever warmth he'd felt toward those surnamed Wescott had cooled.

"It was always my dream," Sequoia said, "as a young child growing up beside the Chesapeake, to go to sea—a calling that even you, as a weekend dabbler, can probably appreciate. My father supported my choice, sponsored me, and paid for my officer's examination. So perhaps you and I aren't too unalike, for we both owe something to our fathers for our successes rather than to any system."

Andrew said without looking at him, "And with your father now in his grave, you seek the paternal devotion of *my* father."

Sequoia very badly wanted to be done with the conversation. "Yours is an impoverished imagination if you think of a few days at a summer home as sponging."

"It's just the timing is rather odd, don't you think? After all these years, for you to just show up out of nowhere."

"What did you say before about people who claim to have seen things that aren't true? I think you called them wrong, and not worth the trouble."

"I was speaking of beliefs, not truth. A belief is whatever one man tells himself. But the truth is whatever two men tell *each other*. I mean, I could tell my father you're here for money and that would be true, wouldn't it? If *he* believed it."

By now the color had returned to Andrew's face. His head rose and he sat straight, rigid and stiff-backed, while he rolled his shirt sleeve back into place. Then he stood and adjusted his clothing.

"I've enjoyed this little chin-wag, cousin. I look

forward to hosting you here on Todeket, weather notwithstanding. See you at dinner. Enjoy your book of fairy tales." He stomped from the room.

Sequoia's uncle was right to protect the Wescotts' privacy, to avoid the locals and pilot their own yachts to and from the island. Who would want stories about madwoman mediums and dipsomaniac dependents swatted around like shuttlecocks every time they went out into the street? Under the public gaze, the ignominies of friends and associates could be pushed aside; the drawbridge could always be raised and the moat waters replenished. But a family only multiplied the humiliations. Family members were just copies and composites of each other, shared noses and hair colors and sensitive stomachs, and the defects of a relation always, in some small way, reflected the defects in ourselves. That's what really mortified us.

The armchair Sequoia occupied had a matching twin, and a broadsheet, folded into quarters, lay on the small table between them. Sequoia picked it up; it was more than a week old. The headlines shouted about three navy ships entering the harbor at Ponce in Puerto Rico without challenge. The commander had threatened to flatten the town, whereupon the Spanish governor, without any means to rebuff the Americans, surrendered. Immediately twelve-thousand soldiers streamed ashore to occupy it.

As he leafed through the newspaper's pages, a sheet

of notepaper fell out. On it was a message written in red pencil, though some of the words were misspelled and the grammar was peculiar.

Dear Sir,

I am sorry we were not properley introduced on the vessle earlier but I am please to make your acquaintince tonight. I have business I wish to discus with you and trust you feel the same.

Yours.

There was no signature.

Sequoia stared at it for a long moment, reading it over several times. He could only assume it'd been left in the newspaper by its previous handler. And yet its contents, no matter how coincidental, seemed particular.

The parlor, lit only by the blurred and dreary light through the wet glass, felt suddenly gloomy and airless, and Sequoia threw down the papers and stalked out.

5

Houseguests occupy unusual spaces in the solar system. They are neither moon nor planet, which at least pursue predictable and regular orbits, and are more like comets, things to be marveled at when they first appear in the sky but soon after ignored.

His hosts, having retreated to various hidden corners and nooks of the house, remained invisible to Sequoia and he considered the best course to integrate himself as he waited for evening. He could return to the bedroom and unpack his belongings into drawers as a statement to his permanence in the house, or he could post himself in some public room to advertise his availability for conversation.

Instead he gravitated to the empty kitchen, where he borrowed a raincoat and hat hanging by the door, donned a pair of rubber galoshes, and went for a walk.

Except for gusts the wind had died and the rain fell straight in droning sheets. The way toward the dock he already knew, so he chose another path of crushed stone. It led through dripping branches that clutched and grabbed at him, somehow injecting water down the back of his neck or up the sleeves of his coat. A tool shed emerged from gloom. Sequoia stepped inside to escape the rain and adjust his coat.

The expected implements hung on hooks or leaned in corners. A threadbare upholstered chair sat next to the window, missing a leg and propped up on bricks. On the windowsill lay a few popular magazines and a stained teacup. A pot for boiling water sat on an ancient wood stove. It wouldn't have merited admission to the Explorers Club, but Sequoia had located what appeared to be the lair of Mr. Burke when he was in retreat from the missus.

Just as he turned to step back into the downpour, a glimmer caught his eye, a single spot of creamy cleanliness in the entire grubby compartment. He reached behind a watering can to withdraw a slim notebook, not much bigger than his palm. Its brown-paper covers were stained with fat black fingerprints, as were some of its leaves; yet the pages were filled with a flowing, feminine hand. Sequoia easily guessed whose dirty fingers had stamped and marred it, and he could imagine Burke sitting in his three-legged chair, idly browsing its contents. But the writing seemed incongruous to that of Mrs. Burke, whom he imagined wrote her shopping lists in crabbed, pinched words. It was a strange thing to find secreted among the shovels and garden shears, and on a sudden impulse, Sequoia jammed it into his pocket and walked out.

His circumlocution of the island continued. Further along he came across a log-beam structure composed of three walls and a sloping roof pitched toward the rear—the fourth wall entirely absent. Around it the rain pooled among the orange needles. Inside, two benches faced a small square cairn of granite cobbles nestled deep in the shadows, a gold-painted crucifix planted upon it like a victorious flag on a mountaintop: the island's chapel, obviating the need to go to Money Island or even ashore for Sunday services. The Wescotts truly were self-sufficient.

A shoe crunched behind him. He turned to see Mr. Burke emerge around the far side of the chapel, watching him.

"Hello," said Sequoia. "I didn't see you there."

Mr. Burke smiled. The rain streamed off him like a Roman statue.

"I was just going for a stroll. Care to join me?"

Mr. Burke's teeth were like big yellow flagstones but no words passed between them. He stood motionless. Sequoia was sure the other man understood him.

Sequoia shrugged and walked on. Every few yards he stopped and turned, and every time Mr. Burke was on the path behind him, maintaining distance between them. Mr. Burke grinned in response.

Unnerved, Sequoia hurried on. He soon ran out of path, ending in a rocky shore where gray waves threw themselves into geysers of spume.

Behind him loomed the house, with its rambling mix of Federalist and Greek Revival and maybe a few more styles too, a motley of eras and additions constructed in a single go. It was like some mansions where the wealthy owner had been to England or France and, full of delight at some ancient mishmash there, returned home with a bag full of drawings and postcards, ready to reproduce the pile stripped of nothing except its context. Some houses are built for utility and some houses for comfort, but some are built for recollection, simply because the lines and gables and cladding brought some happy memory to the owner.

What pleasant reminder the house held for Isaiah Wescott, Sequoia couldn't say, at least based on the tale he'd heard at the saloon. To his eyes, it presented nothing but a meander of missing roof tiles, weathered shutters and moldings, an overgrown yard.

In law there was the phenomenon of *per stirpes*, in which the estate of a deceased man was split evenly among his heirs, usually his children; and if any of his children should have predeceased him, then that child's portion of the inheritance is split evenly among their children. Isaiah Wescott had fathered only two, and Sequoia knew his mother had not inherited any land or houses upon his death. This logic he understood a little; Todeket would've been useless to a woman stranded in Virginia.

But now the son of a Wescott daughter had returned to Connecticut, and *per stirpes*, he wanted his share. Let the Wescotts keep their New York townhouse—Sequoia would take Todeket as his inheritance.

Sequoia turned to watch the waves for a few moments, then retraced his steps toward the kitchen door. This time he found Mr. Burke vanished into the landscape like a rabbit or fox.

As he approached the lean-to chapel, Sequoia's gaze naturally drifted to where he'd spotted Burke, wondering if the man had returned to his starting point. He saw then a very narrow track leading through knee-high weeds, obstructed from view before.

The track curved through the weeds and then past a tight wall of sentinel pines. Beyond, the space suddenly opened into a small field of puddles formed in the pitted slabs of pink granite that formed the island. Scattered at random intervals lay oblong hummocks of rocks piled into cairns.

Sequoia turned to traipse back to the house. Something whooshed past his ear; to his left, a fist-sized stone clapped against the ground and rolled into a patch of weedy grass.

He spun around, knees bent, ready to spring. But he saw no one. Nothing but the rain, droning down relentlessly.

In the kitchen, Sequoia replaced the foul-weather gear on their pegs and took vigil at the window, trying to see where Burke had gone. Questions tripped over themselves in his mind, about why he'd followed him or if Burke had intentionally blocked the path toward that strange and secret little place of stones where he'd nearly been knocked senseless by a flying rock.

"Sequoia, is it? Are you well?"

The day was dense with humidity, yet the speaker was dressed very primly without discomfort in her heavy-lidded eyes or impassive heart-shaped face. In an instant he recognized her as the *other* Mrs. Wescott— the boy Eli's mother.

"Cousin Lisette," Sequoia said, "of course. Yes, I'm well. Why wouldn't I be?"

"You seemed—agitated. Perhaps it was my misinterpretation."

Sequoia gestured toward the window. "This rain, I suppose. Something about it oppresses."

"It's always good to get away from this beastly house," Lisette said with agreement. She put a kettle on the stovetop, and while waiting for it to boil, produced a fan from her apron and fluttered it with a certain languor. "New Haven isn't New York but at times I need to escape to send some letters and have a cup of tea. I usually have Mr. Burke row me to town."

Then, as if in reply to something not said, she added, "I'm making some now. I don't know where Mrs. Burke has gone to—she always seems to just *disappear* when she's wanted. Would you like to join me?"

"No, thank you. I had a cup of coffee earlier."

Lisette said nothing, her expression blank and her gaze distant, and Sequoia wondered if she heard him. Suddenly he remembered the argument earlier and her role as one of the participants, and a wave of embarrassment washed over him.

He tried to think of something to fill the space.

"Are you here for the whole summer?"

Shaken from her reverie, she regarded him as if he'd just climbed down the chimney. "Some years we travel," she said.

The kettle behind her whistled and she turned to transfer it from stove to counter. She then went to a cabinet, found two cups, placed them down, located the strainer and the tea tin, and so on. Sequoia watched her as she conducted each step, her motions neither fast nor slow but methodical and deliberate. Finally, from the same pocket as the fan, she pulled a small vial and, after unscrewing the lid, squeezed four beads of clear liquid from the dropper into one of the cups.

"For my nerves," she said over her shoulder, cognizant the whole time Sequoia watched her. "It's this beastly house. Are you sure I can't interest you in a cup?"

"No, but thank you all the same. May I ask," Sequoia said, "is there a graveyard on the island?"

Lisette smiled a sleepy smile and said, "You've discovered the old cemetery. From colonial times, when Todeket was used to quarantine smallpox victims away from the town. The original part of the house—the part up front—was built as a sort of hospital for them. They'd row them out here and drop them off with a nurse or two. I suppose the nurses were inoculated."

Sequoia frowned. "I thought the house was built by my grandfather after the war. The island was deserted before then."

She shrugged. "I'm just telling you what I've heard. Anyway, I was sent to fetch you. I figured I might as well make a cup of tea while I was here in the kitchen. I don't know where Mrs. Burke is. Before you ask," she said, "I don't have a set number of cups of tea per day. I drink as many as my constitution demands. It's by my doctor's prescription, I promise you. You can imagine that today, with Eli, has demanded a rather heavy quotient."

"I wasn't going to ask. Your health is your own business."

"Andrew would've asked. He has asked already several times today, and will again later, I'm sure. Just watch."

She walked over and offered him a steaming cup and saucer.

"Thank you," he said as he accepted it. "But again, I had a cup of coffee earlier." He placed the saucer on the table.

"You were out in that horrid rain. Don't you want something to warm you?"

"I'm fine, thank you." To change the subject, Sequoia said, "You said you were sent to fetch me."

"Mother wants to see you." The younger Mrs. Wescott sat at the kitchen table, both palms wrapped around her teacup. "But first, Father thought it best if I speak you with beforehand. He's informed us you'll be joining us tonight for the séance."

Sequoia pulled out a chair across from her, the untouched cup between them.

"Your father-in-law told me I should deliver certain answers during it that might pacify our aunt's anguish over Jacob." Sequoia slightly emphasized the word *our*.

"That's right." Lisette sipped her tea, her heavy eyes never blinking, never leaving his face. "The first thing you must understand is there's two specimens of spiritualist. It isn't something openly admitted. The proper reaction, for you, is to be flattered I'm telling you this."

"You're a medium too."

For the first time, she flashed a wicked smile. "Let's have a séance right now, just me and you. *Hark to me, O spirits.*"

A heavy fist rapped upon the kitchen table. Sequoia jumped, despite himself.

"The spirits call you, Mr. Owen." The fist knocked again. Lisette's hands remained upon her cup, her gaze locked upon his with a hungry appetite. The table never jumped. A third bang. The teacup rattled. She seemed to drink Sequoia's confusion and amazement, and that lamia stare disturbed him as much as the noise.

He took a deep breath to calm himself. "I suppose if I was to look under the tablecloth I'd see you've kicked off your shoe. You're knocking your toes against the floorboards."

"I prefer to think of it as knocking on the door of upward progress." She tilted her head toward the doorway to the rest of the house. "I wasn't born into money like them. But I found at a young age I possessed a talent for telling people what they wanted to hear from their departed granny or their dish towel of a dead husband."

"Accompanied by a few theatrics to complete the effect."

"A medium's success is dependent on the novelty of those theatrics. In time mine elevated me into certain rarefied social circles, where an enterprising young woman may, if she so wishes, take her pick of wealthy bachelors."

"How do you do it?" Sequoia asked, intrigued. "I've heard stories. Accounts of musical instruments playing themselves while they float in the air. Personal items dropping out of the ceiling onto the table."

Lisette shrugged. "Please don't mistake my frankness as an obligation to reveal my abilities. I'm telling you this because every séance has a medium, and every medium pulls the strings of her séance. You need to be aware of Geneve's tricks."

"And what about your own?" Sequoia leaned toward her. "Like offering me a cup of tea that you so obviously doped and then switched without me noticing?"

Lisette's eyes darkened. "I don't think I care for your accusation."

"And I don't care for being poisoned. Answer me this: If you and your mother-in-law are in the same profession, aren't you better off with her unemployed? All of high society's ancestors are yours for the gabbing."

"You don't understand how this works," she said. "I love the old dear. We do more business together than apart. I would do the afternoon séances, and she would work the evenings. And if you want us both for a Saturday night? Well, that will set you back."

"So you're partners."

"More or less. Until Jacob died. Since then, with this *Death's black robe* hanging over the family, business hasn't been as lucrative since she moved to Todeket permanently."

"Meaning you haven't been able to pull in more clients on your own. They want *her*."

Lisette scowled. "She's older, more established. When Andrew started courting me, we mutually concluded our talents harmonized. Geneve and I attract overlapping clienteles."

At that moment, a small figure crept into the kitchen and stood beside Lisette. He was much changed since their introduction, dressed in dry clothes with combed hair. To Sequoia, Eli looked no worse for his dunking. The mother reached out an arm to hug him close but her son evaded it, his eyes downcast.

"Can you say hello to your cousin Sequoia?" she asked him.

When Eli didn't immediately respond or even glance

his way, Sequoia said to him, "That's right, we're cousins."

The boy remained silent.

"My mother was sister to your grandfather. That makes your father and me first cousins. You and I are first cousins, once removed."

"He's terribly shy," said Lisette when Eli again didn't answer, a sort of embarrassed awkwardness in her tone. Children are forever the usurpers of propriety, and it's those most concerned with manners whose offspring seem most indifferent to them. She patted his head. "Do you have anything to say to your cousin?"

Eli shook his chin.

"You want your things?"

The boy nodded.

"They're in the drawer in my bedroom. You may go get them." And he scampered from the room.

They waited a moment until his footsteps faded up the back stairs.

Sequoia regarded her. "Clearly you don't believe in the truth of spiritualism. Yet Geneve does. You are a dramaturge but she is sincere. *Very* sincere, at least from what she said earlier."

"She always has been. And since Jacob—well, she *wants* to believe more than ever. The rest of us believe that desire can bring her back. To us." She took one last gulp and set down the cup. "Tea's finished. Let's go see Mother."

As they climbed the front staircase, Sequoia slowed to look around. A strange feeling seized him.

Behind him Lisette asked, "Is anything the matter, Mr. Owen?" Her voice sounded like a smile.

He'd been up and down the staircase twice before, once with Mrs. Burke and then a second time to fetch the Mechanical Oracle. The staircase led up to a landing, with another flight doubling back to the floor above. To his left-hand side ran a chair-rail and skirting board painted in grayish Federal blue. And yet he seemed to remember the stairway curving more, without the skirting board, which was so suggestive of an earlier period.

He didn't drink the tea. But he did drink the coffee.

"No," he said finally. "Just my imagination." The gauzy light inside the house made the details easy to mistake.

6

The elder Mrs. Wescott waited for him in a sitting room off the main bedroom on the second floor. She'd undergone a transformation since their introduction in the kitchen, her hair neatly pulled into a bun, and dressed in a tea gown of white lace and satin with a wrapper the color of forget-me-nots. What astonished Sequoia most was the blossoming—a *return*—of a former charisma. In her gaze lay a certain new sharpness, and to Sequoia it seemed the staggering grandam in the kitchen had been replaced by a much younger, restored edition, her age probably within a score of his own. And yet a certain wildness hid submerged there as well, a kind of thwarted determination soured into obsession. It made him uneasy, that fervency, as if anything he said was just as liable to please her as throw her into a rage.

Past her, through the open door to the bedroom, her pretty nurse Mattie sat working at an embroidery, but of the two, there was no question as to whom was the more magnetic.

"Let me feel your hands, nephew," she said, and she held out her own, palms up. A chair was opposite hers, very close, and Sequoia sat almost knee-to-knee with her to place his hands in hers. Vaguely he was aware that her daughter-in-law, having delivered her package to its recipient, had faded from the room like a dream at breakfast.

Geneve Wescott closed her eyes and massaged the bones of his hands with her thumbs. "Yes," she said, "I can perceive the sympathetic vibrations resonating from your vital force. I see why the spirits gravitate toward you—you, who have nowhere else to go but this house."

Her eyes snapped open. "But you don't believe."

"Of course I do."

"Do you?"

Sequoia withdrew his hands. "You can tell belief from reading my palms?"

"Answer the question."

"No," he said, "I don't believe."

Geneve leaned back in her seat, her lips contracted. "Preston tells me you agreed to sit in on the séance tonight. So why do it if you don't believe?"

Through the doorway, Mattie had paused her embroidery and sat perched on the edge of her chair, a gull on a pile.

For a moment, despite himself, consideration of his uncle's offer deserted him and he answered with a scrap of honesty. "I am sorry about your son and for your loss, and for those reasons alone I'm willing to help."

For a moment, the lady Wescott didn't say anything. "Belief isn't a prerequisite for a séance, Sequoia," she said finally. "In fact, some of my best seances have been with those who *didn't* believe. It's precisely because they're skeptical that the medium can do away with the inessentials of the craft."

"You mean the tricks. Like knocking under the table."

Geneve frowned. "There are varieties of clients, and Lisette works best with the more credulous species. I allow her to winnow the over-trusting in favor of true sensitives."

"Well, I'm not one of them. You couldn't have seen another man on the launch when I picked up your grandson. Only me and the pilot."

"I distinctly saw three figures."

"I'm a sailor, Aunt Geneve, a profession more superstitious than most. But I've always contended superstition was a luxury. We are better dealing with the weather and the conditions as they are."

"More accurately you were a merchant marine. And what is a merchantman but a ferryman, ferrying goods all over the world? Charon ferried souls across the river Styx. Being a ferryman is your use."

Sequoia felt faintly insulted. "Use? I'm afraid I don't know what you mean."

"*Use* is the value we bring to the world. Are you familiar with the works of the philosopher Swedenborg?"

"No."

"Emanuel Swedenborg was a theologian and mystic of the past century," she said. "He originally trained as a geologist, and for years worked as an assayer for the king of Sweden. Then one night as he dined by himself in a tavern, he had a vision." She waved her hands like a lion tamer. "The room darkened around him. A man appeared from thin air, and the light shone on him as if he sat in a spot. The man warned him not to eat too much. Then Swedenborg's vision cleared and he was once more alone. Later, when he went to bed, the man appeared to him again in his dreams and revealed himself as God, and told him he would bestow a new revelation unto him."

"More spiritualism," Sequoia said, the only reply to such a tale. "What then is the concept of *use?*"

"Just that," she said. "God tells us, through his prophet Swedenborg, that order is divine and that by fulfilling our role in that order, we ourselves move in concert with his divine plan. A farmer provides food and milk—and in so doing, is useful to his fellow man. A doctor heals. A soldier defends. Even a streetcar conductor demonstrates use, for he helps people go to where they too will be most useful. You see? It is like a symphony directed by the highest of conductors. Even today, you showed your use by arriving here on the island and saving Eli."

"And I suppose the lazy man is unholy because he does not contribute? As well as the inebriate?"

She beamed. "Brilliant! You grasp Swedenborg's teachings immediately."

"What of the politician? I see little use in most."

"We need them as much as anyone else, for they

help run the nation which protects and nourishes us while we go about our own uses."

In all his years bossing common sailors, listening to graybeards' yarns about mermaids and krakens, Sequoia was hard-pressed to recall anything to match such bunkum. The way of the world was perfect, so sayeth this Swedenborg, and perfection was the way of the world. Under this system, an executioner stood sanctified over the murderer whose throat he neck-tied, all for the difference of a paycheck. Just that morning, as he lingered over his breakfast at the Indian Point House, Sequoia read in the newspaper about an engagement of the previous week, in which a Spanish cruiser was forced aground in Havana Harbor and blown to the waterline by U.S. warships. What *use* had those Spanish sailors demonstrated as steel and gunpowder blasted them into their constituent motes, he wondered.

And then, just as he felt ready to leap up and stride from the room, his aunt Geneve went ahead and said:

"I have taken great solace in Swedenborg's writings over the past year." Her manner was that of the doubter on the cliff precipice, of the not-quite-converted who wants to leap. "I find his theology more comforting than most. He reaffirms Christ's promise of life after death."

The memory of the little island shrine flashed before him and suddenly Sequoia's revolt was pacified. Here then was the vector of the old dame's mental sickness: the worry over her son's immortal soul. Theirs were atheistic times, and only a churl would begrudge a grieving mother some modicum of faith. So what if it was nonsense? The beliefs of ninety-nine percent of the planet, put on a scale, would value less than a pound of manure.

Sequoia leaned close to her. "You saw a man in the boat beside me. You think it was a ghost. And a ghost suggests there is something beyond this life."

"It *proves* it."

In that instant, Sequoia made a decision. He was, as he said, a sailor, and not given much to sailors' superstitions. But he trusted in sailors' intuition, which is a separate thing; the way an experienced sailor can read weather in the clouds or predict storms from the ache in an old injury. He suspected Geneve Wescott possessed something of that intuition also, for she had already guessed a truth she couldn't have possibly known about him.

Sequoia said to her, "May I confess something to you?"

Geneve's eyes regarded him steadily.

"Everything I own in this world is in my carpetbag upstairs." His kept his voice low, too quiet for Mattie in the next room to overhear. "In my pocket lies less than twenty dollars. Every cent I earned from years at sea, everything left to me by my father that wasn't disbursed to my two sisters, is gone. Lost. Taken. Fleeced from me by men who swore on their mothers that I could only profit by my investment, never lose. This world, this *life*, is nothing but a bunco game, meant to swindle every man into starvation. When you say I have nowhere else to go, you cannot possibly understand how right you are."

"You could always return to the merchant trade."

"I cannot. It's barred to me."

"Why is that?"

Sequoia said, "Do you know what a Jonah is?"

When his aunt shook her head, he continued: "A Jonah is someone who has a reputation for being unlucky—someone who brings bad luck onboard ship. I am such a man. For some reason a black mark has been struck next to my name in the cosmic manifest. On a single voyage alone, two men fell from the rigging on separate days, one onto the deck and the other into the sea where he was lost. These were blamed on my presence on the ship. Now no captain will have me aboard, at least those who know my name or face. The only trade I possess is standing in a breadline."

The almost imperceptible expression of indifference to money, possessed only by the rich, fluttered across Geneve's face. "You are family, Sequoia. If you help me and my son," she said, "then you will never worry about your livelihood again."

Sequoia sucked in and released a deep breath, and in that moment his loyalty to this new flag was more complete and total than any patriot who fought before him. He remembered the first gift Anna ever gave him: a small carving knife, to whittle with during his voyages when he was away from her. Its value was trivial, its sentiment priceless. A parallel to his aunt's offer.

"And you want to, what?" he asked. "Contact this spirit, the Todeket Ghost? To ask it about Jacob?"

Geneve's hand latched onto his arm. "*I fear the two are one and the same.*"

Sequoia felt as if she squeezed his heart. "I don't understand."

"Not now." Suddenly she assumed a furtive and suspicious manner. Sequoia turned to look at Mattie, who worked at her needlepoint seemingly indifferent some yards away.

Geneve released her grip on his arm. "I'm so glad we met, Sequoia," she said louder for the nurse's sake. "No matter what *you* believe, I feel you possess an energy conducive to communication across the veil. It would be a comfort if you assisted me tonight."

"It would be my pleasure." Sequoia stood and waved at his clothes, at his worn trousers, old shirt, sweat-stained necktie, frayed jacket. "Except I have nothing to wear to dinner."

"Oh, but you do." Wescott sat up straighter in her chair. "If I'm not mistaken, you are very close in size to Jacob." She reached over to a side table and shook a small handbell. "Mrs. Burke will show you."

The dead son's bedchamber had been preserved as if he was due to arrive on the four-twelve from New York. The sheets were laundered and crisp, the dressing mirror clean, the surfaces dusted, the bottles of cologne arranged immaculately on the bureau. The patterned wallpaper was a deep burgundy, the color of a bruise.

Mrs. Burke presented Sequoia with the contents of the wardrobe, which included a dinner suit that she suggested, as laconically as possible, was appropriate for the evening. She brought him a towel and a pitcher of salty well water, then departed.

Sequoia didn't dress immediately. Instead he wandered the room, picking up hairbrushes and candlesticks before setting them down. A small dish held a few coins, a chipped ceramic marble, a wooden curio retrieved during some trip or voyage. Perhaps the coins held significance, or perhaps they were just the change in Jacob's pocket deposited in the dish before his final hour. Certainly the marble and the curio possessed histories. The dead were always visitants even when not rattling chains and walking through walls, and Sequoia tried to glean something of the man who'd once inhabited the room, if only for a few weeks per summer. Geneve Wescott very much wanted to receive a telegraph from her son, and Sequoia, as the operator delegated to the office, was left to interpret the dots and dashes. How he meant to do so, he had no idea.

An oriel window faced southward over a small writing desk. Sequoia pulled out the chair and sat. How nice it would be to sit at the desk and jot a sentence, he imagined, then stare through the glass at the pines and listen to the waves and the gulls while composing the next line.

Sequoia knew of the Thimbles before his arrival. Years ago he first sighted the islands from the deck of a ship inbound to New York, and speculated if among them stood the house the man at the St. Nicholas Hotel had mentioned. He leaned over the rail to study the isles scattered like dice on a board and asked himself if some family member, some kindred yet stranger, shaded brow with hand and studied him back.

And now there he was, snug among those very same islands. Sequoia always wanted to own an island. It didn't need to be extravagant or even more than a jumble of rocks with a shack on top, but he would hold the deed and it would be his, an island of his own lordship and demesne, where he would tie up his boat and sit in the sun and watch the merchantmen steam by, and wave to the sailors on their decks wishing they were him.

These things he'd meant to do with Anna beside him.

Outside the rain continued to drum down. Absently he continued his examination of the room by pulling open the drawers of the desk. Empty: the life-sized diorama kept by Mrs. Burke didn't extend past initial impressions. The bottommost drawer wouldn't close completely, and as he leaned over to push it shut, a corner or edge bit into his rear. Suddenly he remembered the notebook swiped from Mr. Burke's shack, stuck in his back pocket.

He fanned through its pages. The undated entries

were disjointed, sometimes composed of full sentences and other times just spare notes or ending mid-thought, all written in the same handwriting. A devotional diary of sorts, Sequoia concluded, in which the authoress sketched out letters, or at least notes for them, to no less a correspondent than God, scribbled at odd moments on trains or trams, cut off by arrival at the destination. It was precisely for that reason that the journal was so small and lightweight.

Sequoia checked the clock on the bureau, and perceiving that dinner wasn't for another three-quarters of an hour, turned to the first page and spoke the initial sentence aloud.

"My dearest Jacob has proposed to me, Lord," he read, "and it was with excitement to enter Your Sacrament that I agreed."

7

When Sequoia squeezed into Jacob's dinner jacket, he felt something crinkle against his breast. From the inner pocket he retrieved a piece of paper, folded into thirds. He recognized the handwriting immediately from the letter that fell out of the newspaper in the parlor.

I know yourr intention and I beg you not to follow it threw. I will endure until another comes to displace me. But please have someone else take your seat at the table.

There was neither signature nor mark, just as on the other note earlier. The letter must've remained inside the jacket since before Sequoia arrived on Todeket.

Not knowing what to make of it, Sequoia re-folded the letter and disposed of it inside the nearest drawer. He slammed it shut as if trapping a venomous snake.

Mrs. Burke had reminded Sequoia it was customary for the men of the house to gather in Mr. Wescott's study before dinner, and Sequoia, suddenly feeling like a drink might be the right medicine, quickly descended and knocked on the sliding pocket doors.

The gathering had already begun, the study occupied by Preston and Andrew plus a third man, portly and whiskered but close in age to his uncle. Just as Preston opened his mouth to introduce them, Andrew said, "Is that my brother's suit?"

Sequoia, already self-conscious of the fact that all four cuffs lay north of his wrists and ankles, nodded.

Andrew's face showed the dismay of a hundred social conventions broken like sticks over the knee. "I feel poorly for the tailor to see what's become of his craftmanship."

"Let it go, Andrew," said his father. "What do you expect him to wear? Jacob doesn't need it any longer."

"It's a matter of decorum," said Andrew, "for some distant nobody to come waltzing in here and play dress up in Jacob's clothes."

Sequoia strode over to the stranger and introduced himself.

"John Kynaston," said the man as they shook. "I'm a friend of Preston's."

"More than a friend, I'd like to think," said Preston. "We served in the navy together."

Sequoia said, "I take it you sailed from the city with the Knickerbockers."

"My wife and I came up yesterday from Manhattan on our boat *Navigare Necesse*. Took a little over ten hours," said Kynaston. "I go to my parties, she goes to hers, and we barely see each other for two weeks. It's Eden." He winked.

"Ten hours is a fine time considering the Hell Gate," said Preston.

A certain vertigo struck Sequoia whenever he was introduced to a stranger, only to quickly learn they were an evangelical of some extreme practice or faith.

A pole was thrust into his grip while a hand shoved him onto a wire strung between two pits: on the left, an earnestness to not give offense to the new friend, while on the right yawned skepticism and ridicule. Fortunately Kynaston was something less freakish than either a blue-ribbon pledger or a Seventh-Day cornflake: while Preston and Kynaston had been allies and messmates for decades, it turned out Kynaston's primary aspiration for the evening was to attend the séance. He was a fervent spiritualist.

"I never fail to become possessed during Geneve's soirees," he said to Sequoia. "There was a night about two years ago I cannot ever forget. The room was dark and we were in the midst of summoning the spirits from their sepulchers. 'Hearken to us,' Geneve cried. And then, far off in the distance, I heard the crash of waves. Steadily it grew louder, and then—*boom!* The roar of cannons deafened me. A surge of emotion and valor came upon me in a great wave and I shouted out, 'I have not yet begun to fight!' I could feel planks swaying beneath my feet and instinctively I knew I was on board the *Bonhomme Richard.* Across from me I saw *Serapis*, the union jack flying over her stern. I *was* John Paul Jones. His spirit inhabited me totally, and I relived that day on the North Sea I had read so much about."

"So," said Sequoia, treading carefully among the garden of another man's conviction, "you feel possessed by a different soul? A different mind?"

"I don't just feel it," said Kynaston. "The spirit and

I are united in a single body. I have his thoughts, I have his memories. I have been Jones. I have been the Duke of Wellington. I've been Marcus Aurelius and Hannibal of Carthage. All these spirits have possessed me."

"Truly?"

"Truly. Most truly."

"It's odd that you seem to be possessed solely by the ghosts of famous men. Never the soul of a slave or a commoner."

"Great men have more powerful life forces," said Kynaston. "The vitality of their spirits elbows aside those of lesser beings."

"Here, here," said Preston. "The light of greatness outshines all others."

"What about you, Uncle Preston?" Sequoia eyed him carefully. "Do you believe?"

He didn't answer straight away. "I've never been possessed if that's what you're asking. I remain undecided but open-minded."

Sequoia sipped his whiskey and said to Kynaston, "I take it you read histories for pleasure."

"Exclusively," said Kynaston. "It won't surprise you to learn I'm particularly fond of naval history. I can't understand why anyone reads fiction. You've struck a sore spot of mine—my wife reads novels and it drives me wild. I ask her constantly, 'Why do you bother with that nonsense?' Such a waste of time, filling her brain with things that never happened."

The conversation diverged into historiography, and

for some moments they discoursed upon Francis Park-man, whom Sequoia enjoyed, and Emerson's *Representative Men*, which was unknown to him. He mentally noted to read it.

Their dialogue had the effortless and rolling rhythm of two strangers who share a mutual interest, and throughout both Sequoia and Kynaston tried to contain their excitement as each man happily shouted at the other. Preston punctuated the discourse with his own enthusiasm for the subject, leaving Andrew to stand by in glum silence.

"Here's a bit of history I learned," said Andrew suddenly. "Father, did you know our newfound relation here lost all his money with Midgley and Groves?"

The heads of the other three men revolved to stare at Andrew. Two of them in curiosity, the third with intense animosity.

Andrew swirled the whiskey in his glass. "Turns out Mr. Owen's quite well-known over at their little shoe-shine shop. He lost a considerable sum."

Preston looked gravely at Sequoia. "I'm sorry to hear that, dear boy. Midgley and Groves—" He shook his head. "They aren't known for the prudence of their investments."

"So I learned," Sequoia said. Redness crept across his chest and neck.

"There's no reward without risk," said Kynaston, unperturbed. "Happens to the best of us."

"True," said Andrew. "Isn't it odd, though, how some people can be so knowledgeable about some matters, like books, and yet be so naïve to others, like business?"

"Don't insinuate," said his father.

"I'm not speaking about anyone present. Just a general observation for conversation's sake." He regarded Sequoia with raised eyebrows.

But Sequoia saw from the doubt in Preston's expression the blow had landed. To him the careless drop of a penny into the gutter indicated a certain clumsiness of character, a failure of caution. He'd slipped a rung in his uncle's measure, not so much because of the amount lost but because losing was a defeat and an embarrassment.

Beyond the closed pocket doors drifted the voices of arriving guests. Preston checked his pocket watch and set down his glass, from which, Sequoia noticed, he'd barely taken two swallows. "Time for dinner, gentlemen," he said.

As they shuffled for the doors, Sequoia tapped Andrew on the elbow and said low so Kynaston wouldn't hear, "Hang on a minute."

Preston, however, *did* overhear. "I hope there won't be trouble between you two."

"Not at all, Uncle. I just want a private word with my cousin. Man to man." Sequoia kept his face neutral.

Preston shrugged. "Very well. We'll meet you in the

dining room in less than five minutes." He regarded Sequoia with new misgiving. And then the doors snapped shut behind him and Kynaston.

Andrew stood very straight and alert. "You should know I boxed at Yale."

"That's not what I wanted to ask you."

Andrew watched him with pinched lips.

"Earlier, your mother said something to me. She said she believes the Todeket Ghost and Jacob were one and the same. What did she mean by that? The legend of the ghost goes back decades. Why would she think he's the ghost?"

"I haven't the foggiest."

Sequoia considered. "When did your brother die?"

"Last summer."

Somewhere, a light bell jingled. Mrs. Burke was serving dinner. Sequoia breathed deeply and took a chance. "I found a journal written by the woman Jacob loved. Rachel. I found it in Burke's shed outside. I assume she left it here during a visit and he found it and kept it for himself."

"Impossible," said Andrew. "That girl never set foot on the island. She must've given it to Jacob as a gift and Burke nicked it from his room." His expression darkened. "I don't care for thieves. I will have words with him."

"Their romance must've been serious if Jacob killed himself over it. And yet Rachel never visited the island?"

"No. My parents never invited her."

"Couldn't Jacob invite her?"

"The island belongs to my father. Not Jacob."

The bell insisted, scolding them.

"Why did your parents disapprove?" Sequoia asked.

"Of her? Or the engagement?"

"Either. Both."

"This is ridiculous—dinner is waiting."

"Tell me. It could be important."

Andrew stepped closer and spoke faster, with exasperation, as if explaining directions to a particularly dull pedestrian. "Because they had to. Jacob was always foolish, liable to foolish ideas. He believed in ghosts and Captain Kidd's treasure. And she was an equally foolish girl with a head full of claptrap. So our parents prevented what was a foolish match."

Sequoia said, "Has it ever occurred to you that your parents played a role in his death?"

"I beg your pardon. If a child suffocates from holding his breath because his parents refuse to buy him a taffy, it's scarcely murder."

The bell rang a third time, more furiously. Andrew threw back his head and drained his whiskey, slamming the empty glass onto the desk as punctuation.

"Remember," he said low to Sequoia as they headed toward the dining room, "the objective of the séance is to erase my mother's worries. Jacob is safe and at peace. *That's* what she must understand." Just before they entered, Andrew hissed at him: "If she expects the ghost to possess you, then for God's sake act the part. Tell her Jacob is in Heaven and be done with it."

For all the frantic clanging of the supper bell's uvula against brass, Sequoia and his cousin were not the last to arrive to the dining room. In addition to the family members and the nurse and Kynaston, a new couple was also present, whose given names Sequoia forgot ten seconds after their introductions. Mr. Tracy struck him as having entirely too many teeth in his mouth and was so stiff and sober-faced Sequoia assumed his money was made in the mortuary business, while his chirpy restless wife reminded him of a robin dancing for worms in a yard. Spiritualism and sailing attracted a range of personalities.

None had taken their seats due to a crucial absence among the room's inhabitants. Mrs. Burke rang the bell once again, a single sharp peal. On cue, the door on the far side of the room opened. In walked Geneve Wescott.

Her husband visibly rocked on his heels, which was, Sequoia supposed, the intended reaction. She wore a pale shamrock gown with great puffy leg-of-mutton sleeves, a choker of silver and small emeralds at her throat. Recovering himself, Preston stepped up to her and, clasping her hands in his own, told in her low tones how astonishing and ravishing she was. Andrew agreed more loudly.

She, meanwhile, resisted their compliments and commendations, denying her worth. The obvious pleasure with which she did so betrayed any ounce of sincerity.

Sequoia and the rest watched this spectacle of flattery, their own mumbled praise like individual claps drowned in the crowd's ovation. His glance happened to land upon the nurse Mattie, standing just behind her charge, only to find she already regarded Sequoia with an intent yet inscrutable expression. She quickly looked away.

They sat at their plates in a radiation of awkwardness. The table persevered through courses of little-neck clams and cold soup with small talk of inconsequential things, buoyed by plenty of long pauses as spoons were brought to mouths. No one could find in their pockets the flint and steel to spark more than ten words.

Any guest in someone else's house has a distinct advantage: namely, the vanity of the host. Every homeowner loves to discuss his house and furnishings, and it just so happened that upon entering the room, Sequoia's eye was arrested by a portrait on the wall behind his uncle sitting at the far end of the table. The subject, a black-haired young woman in a scarlet dress of indeterminate period, regarded the room with a stern expression. Her one hand rested on the back of an upholstered chair, and in the other—and, for some strange reason, this is what piqued Sequoia's interest— she clutched a horsetail flyswatter.

"Uncle Preston," asked Sequoia, "who is that in the painting behind you? A great-grandmother of mine?"

Preston turned to glance over his shoulder. "I have no idea," he said, and laughed.

"You mean the painting is so old you've forgotten her name?"

"No, Sequoia," said Geneve to his left. "He means the woman is no relation to any of us."

Before Sequoia could ask further, Preston explained. "That portrait," he said, "was one of the souvenirs my father brought home from the last war. He and some men came across an old abandoned plantation house somewhere in the marshes of the Carolinas, and as no one seemed to want it, my father cut it from the frame, rolled it up, and brought it home as a keepsake. We keep it here in memory of his service to our country. Who the woman is, I cannot say."

Sequoia said, "That's very strange. The story I've heard was that the plantation wasn't abandoned," and he proceeded to summarize the tale as he'd learned it from the shellbacks at the saloon, in which Isaiah Wescott and his marines, having discovered the hidden house deep on a swampy island, found it very much inhabited and looted it in retribution for the old woman's betrayal.

"For a Virginian who's never been north before, you do know more about us than you let on, don't you?" said Preston. "I cannot say what the truth is, only echo the story as it was told to me." He stabbed his fork at the whitefish on his plate. "But I will say that in conflict, all is fair, so I see no dishonor even if the house was still occupied."

"I think there's a big difference between searching a home for necessary supplies and victuals in a time of war," said Sequoia, "and ransacking it like burglars for works of art."

"You Southerners are all puffed-out chests and no sense," said Andrew. "Calling my grandfather a thief—a man you never even met."

Sequoia leveled his gaze at him. "*Our* grandfather. I'm only saying that war encourages looseness of morals."

"I've always assumed," said Geneve, "that the woman in the painting was the same who shot your father, Preston."

"Really, Geneve." Disappointment saturated Preston's tone. "I'd like to think this whole time we haven't been presided over by his would-be murderer."

Mr. Tracy said with a cocked eyebrow, "This is your first time above the Mason-Dixon, Mr. Owen?"

"My uncle exaggerates. I've been to New York as a merchant marine. I was born here in Connecticut but raised in the Commonwealth of Virginia."

"Is that so?"

"What do you mean a *looseness of morals*?" said Andrew.

"Simply as I put it," Sequoia said. He set down his cutlery on the plate. "That by giving permission to commit the singular act which in every other situation is anathema—to take a life—it is not a very far stretch to permit lesser crimes as well. We hear stories of the Hessian mercenaries during the Revolution and how they were feared and loathed as bandits. But who can blame them? Shanghaied and shipped across the Atlantic by their princes, ordered to attack people with whom they had no quarrel, all for the pleasure of officers and politicians who cared not a whit for their lives." Sequoia felt a little drunk. "Why shouldn't they steal a few silver buttons or shoe buckles for their trouble?"

"You cannot compare American soldiers and sailors to Hessians, whose bellicosity is natural to their German blood," said Andrew.

Preston said, "I take exception to your characterization of officers not caring about their men."

"Quite," said Kynaston.

"Most officers feel great compassion toward the men under their command," said Preston. "Take the letter that appeared in Thursday's papers. I can think of no better testament to compassion than the officers risking their commissions and careers on behalf of their men's health."

The letter, which had been submitted to the commander of the Fifth Corps a week ago, had been written and signed by a number of the commander's top officers in Cuba. They warned the soldiers currently stationed in Santiago after the city's fall were too weakened by yellow fever to withstand the upcoming malaria season. The officers projected deaths in the thousands, and pleaded for the Corps to be transferred from Cuba to the United States so that they might recover.

"Appalling conditions," said Mattie. "To think of four-thousand men sick with fever."

"They must be evacuated immediately," said Mrs. Tracy. The rest of the table agreed.

Sequoia said, "On the contrary, Uncle, the fact that the letter was delivered to the newspapers only affirms the writers knew their request would be denied and they hoped to rally the American public to their position."

"That seems hardly likely since by the time we citizens read the letter, the order had been already given to bring them north."

"It should've been done earlier. Or, better yet, the soldiers should've never been sent to Cuba in the first place."

Mattie said, "You sound as if you're against the war, Mr. Owen."

"I am. Very much so."

Andrew laughed as if Sequoia had slipped on a banana peel. "How stupid. The war is practically over."

"Just because we've won doesn't diminish the argument against starting it in the first place."

"We didn't start it. The Spanish did."

"I'm shocked to hear you express opposition," said Preston. "I must say, I find that attitude very callous toward the suffering Cubans. Their treatment at the hands of the Spanish has been nothing less than barbaric—the *reconcentrados* forced from the countryside into towns where they starve or die of disease. Hundreds of thousands slaughtered."

"I don't doubt the horror of the Cubans' situation," Sequoia said. "Only the legitimacy of our involvement. As they say, truth's diminution is a calamity of war. Above all I value truth. It often strikes me, as someone who has never experienced the terror and privation of it, how those who have survived war can still be proponents of it afterward."

Preston dabbed his mouth with his napkin. "You believe because I am a veteran I should protest all other wars."

"In a walnut shell, yes."

But the old man shook his gray head. "I don't see it like that. Living through war is difficult for any soldier and sailor, I agree, but I must stress how important it is for a young man. Much of the success in my career is to be attributed to my service during the rebellion, from the friendships I made in the navy," he nodded at Kynaston, "and to the approbation and respect I was given afterward by employers and bankers and even merchants in the street. You suggest war is nothing but fear and hardship, and I agree partly: it *is* those things. But from the moment surrender was accepted, I've experienced nothing but good fortune. This, I think, is the true difficulty of your generation—that we do not have *enough* war. Just this morning, I read in the newspaper about a man who accidentally overdosed on opium in a hotel. Last week there was a story about a man who did so on purpose because he was unlucky in business. This species of tragedy was unheard of in my youth. I fear that without knowing death, my grandchildren's generation will grow to maturity with a lesser value of life. On the contrary, Sequoia," he said, "not only I am *not* against the current war against Spain, I chide its brevity. If only Germany would join forces with the Spaniards so that it might be prolonged! Then could Andrew and his mates, and perhaps you too, be extended the opportunities and principles that were granted me some thirty-odd years ago."

A strip of ignited magnesium could hardly have burned hotter than Sequoia at the end of this speech. Here was Preston Wescott, a man by hook or crook or perhaps just dumb luck found himself alive at the end of the war with all limbs and faculties intact, and yet also assumed that fact to be trifling. Like a gambler who, through the merit of a few winning cards thrown in his direction or gravity stopping a wheel on the number of his sweetheart's birthday, confuses a fluke for talent, he imagined his enlistment on a tub—doing what, exactly, besides eating bad food? blockading a harbor? running dispatches?—qualified him as an authority on the rosy benefits of nations sending their own citizens to murder and spoliate. *What an awful family this is*, Sequoia thought, *of mad women and louche men*, and he swore at himself for ever dawdling more than five minutes past their threshold.

He considered throwing down his fork and knife

and swimming to shore when Lisette said to her mother-in-law, "Have you ever tried to contact her?" She gestured toward the woman in the painting.

Geneve pinched the emeralds at her neck. "I've never thought about it. She would be difficult to contact without knowing her name."

"But that's just it," said Lisette in her sleepy drawl. "You could ask her, and we'd finally know who she is."

Teasing or not, Geneve entertained the idea. "I must say, the more I consider the possibilities Swedenborg has revealed to me, the more I become excited to speak again with the spirits."

She addressed her guests. "You see, beyond death Swedenborg tells us that men and women become spirits. After a period of seasoning in which spirits become truer realizations of their characters—either good or evil—those good spirits are instructed by angels on how to better themselves so that they may enter Heaven. There they too shall become angels, for Heaven is infinite, and there is an infinity of labors for them to complete. It would be fascinating to ask the woman in the painting where she stands in the process. Has she transitioned to an angel yet, or is she still a spirit? I wonder."

The believers nodded and debated the issue through the stewed mushrooms and roasted turkey.

Too angry to speak, Sequoia studied the portrait with deep interest, very much in contrast to Mattie opposite him, her eyes averted as if it depicted Medusa.

His gaze darted from the painting to Mattie's face and back again, at the nose and high forehead and widow's peak.

"If you ask her spirit anything," Sequoia said finally, "ask her about the flyswatter she's holding. She looks as if she's about to smack the painter with it."

"If she's the same woman, then she certainly had a crack at my father," said Preston.

"The truth is the old woman shot Isaiah with a pistol," Geneve said to Sequoia. "The bullet cut through his scalp. He told me the story himself."

"Before or after he died?"

Suddenly Lisette Wescott screamed.

Every gaze shot toward her. Sequoia nearly leapt to his feet. Lisette sat with her napkin pressed to her mouth, shoulders quivering.

She was laughing.

Andrew drank from his wine glass and peered darkly at his wife. "How many cups of tea have you had today, Lisette?"

Taking her own glass stem in hand, she swirled its contents and sipped. "Even someone with such terrible eyesight as you can see I'm drinking wine," she said, and the triumphant glance she cast at Sequoia, across the table, was that of the haruspex whose divination has come true.

"Drink up, cousin," she said, and Sequoia, to rinse the disgust from his mouth, grabbed his glass and downed its contents entirely.

8

Through the parlor window lay the former front yard. Sequoia thought of it as *former* because in some previous era the trees were razed to create a lawn where one might throw down a picnic blanket or swat a ball through a wicket; but through negligence the surrounding pitch pines had reclaimed their bygone lands like so many rebellious sepoys. The invading saplings reached no taller than a man so the yard's boundaries could still be delineated, and clumps of grass, grown tall and feral, poked through rugs of needles.

After dinner the party retired to the parlor for coffee and port, although thankfully, because Geneve didn't allow smoking in her house, there were no cigars—the smoke would've thickened the atmosphere unbearably. Sequoia refused alcohol, and he noted that Lisette also drank only coffee but without any additives, or at least none he spotted.

The rain, having finally quit, brought in its absence a magnifying effect of the atmosphere. In breaks of conversation the waves threw themselves furiously against the stony shore, and the volume of the noise made it seem like they washed against the foundation of the house. A cold front followed the storm, and in the cooler air, fingers of mist began to curdle from the earth and stone baked by the summer heat. The humidity was intense.

The discussion stayed light and frivolous. The parlor was home to the family gramophone and Lisette played several records like "A Hot Time in the Old Town," "Orange Blossoms," and "Mister Johnson Don't Get Gay." No one bothered to talk to Sequoia, leaving him free to boil undisturbed in an armchair.

For his life, he couldn't understand what came over him at dinner. He hadn't drunk that much and yet a lightheadedness overcame him, a giddiness. The success of his plan depended, of course, on remaining agreeable and congenial to all of his new relations; but at dinner he couldn't let go of his point regarding the war. He should've nodded his head, mumbled compliance, and let the topic pass. Instead a kind of contempt and judgment simmered up inside him, the foam spilling over the edge of the pot, uncontrollable, and it was only because Lisette and Geneve changed the subject that Sequoia hadn't exploded outright.

On the wall between windows hung a pair of pistols, while on an end table rested a stiletto of a knife, probably used as a letter opener. He recalled the cutlass in the office, and felt like a balloon in a house of needles.

Sequoia could see now what as a child was always opaque. Raised among wreckage, frequently witnessed and yet rarely discussed, his antipathy to war, in senses both general and specific to the nation's current adventure, was the unintended result. Growing up, every family in eastern Virginia had some tale of woe, some relative who didn't come home or some experience with loss and privation. But to children born during or after it, the war seemed as distant as the events of the Bible, a battle between gray-haired patriarchs over issues just as antediluvian. Whenever Sequoia sat in the pew and listened to the minister droning on about Abraham's binding of Isaac, he thought to himself what an imbecile Abraham was, ready to plunge the dagger into his own son's breast on the basis of faith; and yet more ludicrous still did the tariff of 1828 and John Brown sound as rationales for taking up arms.

Sequoia's father stood by his principles, and what had they brought him? Dissension and alienation from his wife's family, political ruin, exile from his home state to the edge of the Chesapeake, where he built a modest shipping business by simple merit of bringing a bit of capital into a land subdued into poverty.

For the losers, nothing had been gained by the war but very much squandered, and yet while growing up the conversation at the supper table occasionally loitered on lost causes and if only this or that happened instead. Sequoia came to equate war with waste, a garbage till that old people fought over until they fell down and decomposed and added to the refuse, their bitterness and disappointments just another compost layer. War was stupid, and by extension so were its proponents.

But tonight he'd supped with the victors for a change. For them war was the memory of a childhood

Christmas when they received everything on their lists. Decades later, bullets and disease were misremembered as a glorious party, and those who fell, their blood spurting from too many cuts and out all the wrong holes, were regarded as old acquaintances who'd moved to some other state and stopped writing. It enraged Sequoia, his uncle's exaltation of it.

And yet staking so much on his own opinion was, in a sense, to become a combatant. If war was pointless, Sequoia told himself, then perhaps so was having a point of view about it. It shouldn't bother him if his neighbors wanted to sound a bugle and march into a hail of Spanish lead, as long as they didn't carry him off to Havana on their shoulders.

Outside of Sequoia's head, thoughts of battlefields stalked far from the parlor as the atmosphere pressed heavily against them. Mrs. Tracy and Mattie sat gabbing on a couch, furiously fanning themselves, while Mr. Tracy and Andrew stood by the door, hoping for the slightest breath of air blowing from the open front door in the hallway beyond. Kynaston perched on the edge of a chair, rubbing his belly and sweating liberally.

"Indigestion, John?" asked his host.

Kynaston blotted his forehead with a handkerchief. "Too much rich food," he replied. "I always overeat at your table. Mrs. Burke's fine cooking."

"A bit more port will settle you," said Preston and he topped his friend's glass from the bottle.

On a low table between them, Preston had set up

the Mechanical Oracle and with Sequoia's permission demonstrated it for Kynaston. It delighted the other man.

"Oracle," said Kynaston very loud as if the machine was hard of hearing, "will the séance tonight allow a spirit to enter me?"

The reels spun, then snapped into place. Preston read the reply: "*A possibility must remain concealed. Your future will be revealed.*"

At this punchline, the two men burst into laughter. "That one rhymed!"

"Clever, very clever," said Kynaston, first to the Oracle, then repeating the words to Preston and Sequoia separately, as if it was a new thought each time.

Geneve, sitting by herself, watched this exchange through narrow eyes, and her husband, perhaps nicking his thumb on the rusty steel in her gaze, asked her if she also found the mechanism cunning.

"It's a foolish contraption," she said. Then, in a more conciliatory tone toward Sequoia, she added, "although I concede the ingenuity of its design."

"Don't worry, Geneve," said Preston. "It's far too small to put you out of business."

Geneve's neck straightened like an angry goose. "Why on earth would you think I have anything to fear from a box of rivets? Of course it won't put me out."

"And even if it did," said Kynaston, "we always need someone to operate the machines."

For Preston this was a joke too far, and he smiled

politely while keeping his gaze on his wife, whose eyes flashed like sparks off a grinding wheel.

During this exchange, Lisette hovered near the phonograph, swaying very slightly to its crackling tune. Her eyelids, nearly closed, slid upwards and she said to Geneve, "The value we provide is deeper than the message, dear. The spirits always need interpreters for their omens and advice."

Geneve turned halfway in her seat to regard her daughter-in-law with something of a cowled glare. "Speak for yourself, Lisette. I perform a service greater than just interpretation. I am a summoner and diviner." She sat straight again. "You will see. Tonight we'll learn the truth about Jacob. Tonight we summon the Tode-ket Ghost."

"*Ghosts*," said Sequoia.

Geneve pivoted to stare at him. "What?"

"Ghosts, plural." Sequoia, roused from his sulking, lifted his head. "The eyewitnesses in the album report seeing a different figure each time, male and female. Never the same ghost twice."

"Bosh," said Geneve. "The legend always speaks of a single spirit. *The* ghost."

"A witness sees only one ghost at a time," said Sequoia, "but clearly there's multiple."

"Utter rot." Geneve's face reddened, from heat and anger. Tears welled in her eyes.

"Why is it so important?" Lisette pretended to adjust some part of the phonograph. "Perhaps Cousin

Sequoia is right. How does that change anything?"

Geneve slapped the arm of her chair. "Because it's the *principle*. It's pointless to continue if we cannot agree on basics. Here, Sequoia," she said, addressing her nephew, "you said at dinner that above all, you value truth."

Sequoia, with reluctance, answered. "Yes. I did say that."

"Then mustn't the pursuit of truth also be valuable and worthwhile?"

"I suppose so."

"But, cousin," said Lisette, speaking now to him, "by that reasoning, wouldn't resistance to facts, the refusal to believe something you don't like—by that rationale, isn't the protraction of a falsehood just as valueless? Harmful, even."

Like an animal in a snare, he saw no escape. "I guess that's right too." He considered chewing off his own leg and leaping out the window.

But unlikely salvation walked over to lay a reassuring hand on his mother's shoulder. "Both ideas can coexist for the moment," said Andrew. "But perhaps tonight, we'll gain some clarity in the matter." Then he turned to his wife. "Really, Lisette, does it pain you so much to show my mother even a scintilla of respect?"

"I said nothing disrespectful."

"Right there. *Right there*," said Andrew. "You can't let anything be spoken without contradicting it. Least of all anything Mother says."

Geneve reached to her shoulder and squeezed Andrew's hand in her own.

Lisette said, "So any disagreement I make is regarded as being disagreeable."

"You're doing it again." Andrew shook his head in exasperation. "It's maddening, I tell you."

A round table stood in the center of the room, at which a cushioned armchair had been placed as well as five other armless chairs. Everyone seemed to purposefully ignore the arrangement, as if coming too close would cause the furniture to scatter and run like a herd of deer, and so the partygoers gravitated toward the edges.

With an audible clink, Geneve dropped her coffee cup on its saucer and stood. "It's time to begin," she said and swept toward the armchair, closing all discussion with firm punctuation.

Lisette returned the gramophone's needle to its cradle. The faces of the other guests betrayed their expectation.

"Sequoia, if you please," said Geneve, indicating the chair to her right, as anticipated.

She scanned the rest of the room with a level gaze.

"Mr. and Mrs. Tracy," she said, "if you would care to join me, I would be most grateful. And Mattie as well." She looked in the direction of her husband and Kynaston. "And of course it wouldn't be a proper séance without you, John."

The guests moved to take their chairs, Mrs. Tracy's

skirts bouncing as she kicked her heels in a near sprint. Kynaston beamed as he wiped the sweat from beneath his collar.

Andrew started forward. "Mother, one of the family members should be present at the table."

"So there is," she said. "Your cousin Sequoia."

"But surely—" He stopped to rephrase his thoughts. "We all realize you intend to contact Jacob. Don't you think Father or I or even Lisette, those people who knew him so well—shouldn't one of us be among those who reach out to him? Not—forgive me…" He looked at the guests. "Not strangers."

"Who but his own mother," Geneve said with coolness, "could be closer to him? I cannot imagine a bond stronger between two souls as that of mother and child." She threw glances at Andrew and Lisette. "Tonight we will attempt an *honest* séance, free from tricks or deceptions."

"I have to insist. One of us must sit at the table."

"And as the medium, I insist that I choose the participants."

"Please, dear," said Preston. "Allow Andrew to sit at the table. It means so much to him."

"What is this?" Geneve stared at her husband and son, lips barely covering a snarl. "Am I to be questioned and thwarted at every juncture? I am the *medium*."

Preston immediately relinquished. "Of course, my dear. Don't let it upset you." And with a look, Andrew likewise withdrew his petition.

Shades were pulled, curtains drawn, the lamps extinguished save for a lonely candle on the table. Sequoia expected incense, the association between Eastern spices and mysticism large in his sailor's mind, but he was disappointed.

"Get the board, Lizzy," said Geneve. "Tonight we shall use the board."

Lisette returned from somewhere with a large panel of wood, painted with the alphabet and a row of single-digit numbers. In the corners were the words *YES* and *NO*. She laid this on the table, along with a triangle of wood set upon tiny steel casters.

Geneve ordered every participant to lightly lay both forefingers on the planchette.

The séance began with a great deal of hailing of the spirits. Entreaties and invitations were called out, followed by utterances from Geneve that Sequoia recognized as bits of Hebrew, Latin, and French, although what these words and phrases were, he had no idea. Neither, he suspected, did anybody else—least of all, the medium.

"Spirit of Todeket," asked Geneve, "are you with us?"

The candlelight illuminated only the board and the twelve disembodied hands that emerged from the darkness. No light came through the windows; the faces of Sequoia's co-supernaturalists lay buried beneath shadows.

"Ghost of Todeket. Are you here?"

Like the rest, the pads of Sequoia's index fingers rested lightly on the planchette. Any attempt to push or pull it was resisted by the pressure of ten other digits squeezed onto its edges. Impossible, he thought, to manipulate an answer to any one person's inclination.

And yet to his amazement, the planchette dragged his fingers toward a corner of the board. *YES*, it read.

A tremor of excitement ran through the circle.

"Spirit," said Geneve, "we thank you for preserving our grandson Eli earlier today. We thank you for aiding our nephew Sequoia Owen in his rescue."

The planchette sat motionless.

"You cannot know what relief your presence brings. The prophet Swedenborg tells us that neither spirits nor angels can be perceived by those on Earth, and therefore they communicate to us by indirect means."

Sequoia could tell Geneve was steeling herself, gathering the courage to speak the riddles closest to her heart.

"Spirit, I believe you are a guardian of this house, assigned to watch over all its inhabitants and keep us safe. Is this true?"

For a moment nothing moved. Then slowly the planchette drifted to the opposite corner. *NO*.

Sequoia noticed his mouth had become very dry.

Geneve asked in a small voice, "Is my son Jacob with our Lord?"

The planchette swirled in a circle, arriving back to where it started. *NO*.

A short, stifled sob. Geneve lifted her hands to her face.

"My dear," said Preston. "We need to stop this."

"Be silent." Geneve shook her hands and returned them to the planchette.

The planchette moved again, this time toward the alphabet. First to the *S*, then *H*, then *E*.

"*She?*" asked Mrs. Tracy. "Who is she?"

It spelled again, flowing smoothly between the letters. *SHE DIED.*

The air around Sequoia seemed to hum like a piano wire and the hair on the back of his neck stood on end. He felt as if he conspired with witches, seated around a cauldron that boiled with hellfire.

Geneve's tone became demanding. "Spirit, we do not understand. Who died?"

But the planchette sat motionless. Somewhere Kynaston mumbled, "You may see by our colors we are no pirates," but everyone ignored him.

"I will ask again. *Who* died?"

The planchette wobbled on its coasters, shivering and shaking. Like a mouse it took off across the board, back and forth, so fast that Sequoia could barely keep his fingers on it. It felt alive.

SHE DIED, it spelled. *SHE DIED SHE DIED SHE DIED.*

It stopped briefly. Then, as the séancers panted like runners after a trolley, it spelled a new message. *MUR-DERED.*

Sequoia couldn't breathe, the air crushed from his windpipe. He clawed at his neck, only to find fingers already there, wrapped around it.

Fingertips pressed into his larynx. He dug his nails into them, tried to pull them away. It was impossible, like poking at steel cables. Thumbs pressed into his spine at the base of his neck.

Around him the others babbled. *Who died? She died. Who is she? I don't understand.* Completely ignorant of him in the near-total blackness.

He slammed his fists into the gloved hands around his throat. In another few seconds, his esophagus would collapse completely. Thrashing in his seat, he reached backward and upward to swing and flail against the body he knew was behind him. His hits connected without effect, no force behind them.

"Mr. Owen," said Mattie somewhere to his right, "please sit still."

"He's having a fit," Kynaston said. "The spirit is in him!"

Stars popped at the edge of Sequoia's vision—he was blacking out.

Sequoia raised his legs and planted his feet on the table's edge. He shoved backward. His head slammed into the body behind him to push it away. The grip broke at the thumbs, the weakest point. Sequoia and the chair crashed to the floor.

Across the room, the Mechanical Oracle, untouched by anyone, spun its reels.

Immediately the room turned over. Lights erupted and, half-blinded, hands flew across eyes. Preston and Andrew jumped to their feet, and Mr. Tracy, not understanding what was happening, leapt up too, knocking his chair over. Kynaston, drenched in sweat, rose and stumbled around the room. Mrs. Tracy pulled at the neckline of her dress, face flushed.

Sequoia rolled off the chair to his knees, clutching his throat. He breath came in loud rattling wheezes. The others stared at him without comprehension.

John Kynaston—eyes bulging from a face red as sunset—suddenly said, "Damn you, Blackbeard, surrender in the name of his majesty" and threw himself across the room at some invisible foe. Then, grasping his chest as if stabbed, he collapsed onto the floor.

9

Sequoia lay on the bed in the garret bedroom stripped to his waist, the air dense enough to cut with his pocket-knife. Not a puff of air moved in the room. Outside the waves crashed against the rocks, amplified through the open window like a gramophone horn.

A mist of drowsiness hovered at the edge of Sequoia's vision but sleep escaped him. The sheets lay wet and clammy under his skin, and in the candlelight—the vertical flame of the candle never budging from its axis—he traced the cracks in the ceiling plaster, and in his head.

As extraordinary as the séance was, John Kynaston's collapse overshadowed the attack on Sequoia. Mattie knelt on the parlor floor and held Kynaston's wrist and pulled at his eyelids, only to pronounce the sentence with a head shake. His sailor's heart, pierced by Blackbeard's cutlass onboard the deck of an imaginary *Jane*, had burst. Preston would not accept the news, clutching his dead friend's hands in his own while he sobbed, until finally Andrew gently clasped him by the shoulders and pulled him away so that Sequoia could drape a tablecloth over the body.

There was little to do until morning. Not knowing the whereabouts of the now-widowed Mrs. Kynaston, and recognizing the authorities on land likely tossed and turned in their own sweat-soaked beds, Andrew and Sequoia lifted Kynaston onto the sofa and resolved to act at sun up.

The Tracys abandoned ship immediately. Spiritualists or otherwise, the manifestation of literal death proved too much and they fled the island as soon as the corpse settled into the couch. Thick fog proved no obstruction. Like Romans evacuating under Vesuvius's glow, they cast off their dinghy and disappeared completely. Whether they would ever be seen again by mortals Sequoia didn't know, but he was sure he'd never again lay eyes upon them.

The fog closed around the island as their oars faded, sealing those left behind as completely as butterflies under glass. The family retreated to the kitchen.

Excitement killed Kynaston, that was easy enough to see. But who then tried to strangle Sequoia? The only men not seated at the table were Preston and Andrew, and he hardly believed his uncle capable of it. And Andrew remained unconvinced that nothing more sinister had occurred than Sequoia swallowing a chicken bone or his own tongue.

At least until a bruised ring of purple appeared around Sequoia's neck.

"It was the ghost itself that tried to claim you," said Geneve. "It spoke of murder."

"It was no spirit," said Sequoia. His voice was

choked and raspy. "It was the hands of a man, gloved in black leather."

"Come off it," said Andrew. "Not one of us saw anything or heard anything. It wasn't a man and it certainly wasn't a ghost."

"The room *was* very dark," said Lisette.

"So what are you implying?" Andrew said to her. "That someone else, some stranger, entered the room and attacked him? Preposterous."

"*It was the ghost,*" said Geneve. Her tone was firm, even irritated. "I was wrong to summon it. The presence of the island spirit always accompanies calamity and death. Sequoia's life was the price to be paid for its appearance. But in the end, he survived. John did not."

Preston slumped in dejection at the table, a glass of brandy before him. "And where do you suppose he is now, Geneve?"

For moment Geneve didn't answer. Then, without looking at anyone, she said, "Where all souls go when they die on Todeket. They must provide *use.*" And she rose and excused herself, commenting on how very tired she was.

Now in his guest room, sleep wouldn't come. Over and over the zoetrope of the séance replayed in his memory as Sequoia tried to recall every word and detail. He remembered a terror seizing him as the planchette moved and spelled out words—a kind of exhilaration like climbing into the highest rigging and peering down at the ship and seas rocking beneath him, that same sense of distance and vertigo.

Every few moments he sipped from a glass of warm brandy and water beside his bed, his throat sore and constricted.

Had something entered him and spoken through his fingertips on the planchette, *possessed* him as John Kynaston described? The man said he'd never failed to become possessed at Geneve's séances. What did that even mean, Sequoia wondered—like being so drunk he couldn't recall the night before, and yet somehow his own body was piloted through the streets and back to its berth. Who stood at the tiller when the captain and navigator lay too blotto to command?

Maybe it was that fact, even when memory stopped stamping its ink onto the pages, when the feet still continued to walk, no matter how they stumbled, and the tongue still continued to speak, no matter how it slurred, that was the easiest and simplest evidence of the soul.

Someone tapped on the bedroom door. Sequoia rose and hastily buttoned a shirt before cracking it open. Mattie stood in the hall, her face lit by the light of a single candlestick.

"Everyone else is asleep."

He waved her inside and shut the door. Due to the angles of the ceiling there weren't many places for either of them to stand, so she perched herself on the edge of the single wooden chair. Sequoia sat on the bed.

"I've been meaning to talk with you," she said, "ever since supper."

He knew immediately what she meant, or at least thought she did. "You refer to the resemblance between you and the portrait in the dining room? I speak plainly."

She didn't look at him directly, instead presenting her profile in the half-light. If anything, the affinity struck even more strongly than before: the dark eyes, the hairline, and above all, the removed and haughty demeanor.

"I actually don't know who the woman in the portrait is," said Mattie. "Like your family, I'm not sure if it's my great-grandmother or not. That's what's been lost, the knowledge of how I connect to the plantation and to my past. My heritage."

Sequoia shook his head. "What I don't understand is why none of them see it."

"It's because you have fresh eyes. They met me outside of this house, in New York away from the portrait. By the time I came here to live with Mrs. Wescott, I had already calcified in their arrangement. I was Mattie Fuller the nurse—not Mattie Fuller *Desole*, descendant of the Desoles of South Carolina. They see the role I play, not the person."

"It beggars the imagination to believe your presence in this household is a coincidence."

Her shoulders moved in the barest suggestion of a shrug. "Providence brought me here. I like to think the soul of my dead great-grandmother has guided my actions."

"Are you even a nurse?"

"I have some medical training," she said. "I was raised in an orphanage that taught its girls useful skills. Nursing a madwoman takes very little talent, I assure you. Soothing her anxieties mostly, with assistance from the occasional shot or tablet in my kit. Which is why," she said, "I needed to talk to you."

She reached into her pocket, then held a fist toward him. Her opened hand revealed a half-dozen glass ampoules, all empty.

"The Keeley Cure," said Sequoia.

"I found these in the drawing room in a vase on the mantel. As if someone wanted to hide them."

Sequoia plucked a vial from her palm and turned it over in his fingers. "You're saying this is what killed John Kynaston."

"I think in the port Mr. Wescott served him before the séance."

"No." Sequoia shook his head. "It's impossible my uncle would murder his best friend."

"Of course not. He was as unknowing as the victim. It was someone else."

"Then who? And for what purpose?"

Mattie regarded him steadily. "The same person who suggested that someone must die whenever the ghost appears."

Sequoia rose to his feet. "My aunt may be mad," he

said, "but there's nothing to suggest she's a murderer."

"Mr. Kynaston meant nothing to her—simply a friend of her husband's. Don't you see? His death proves the truth of the curse she believes in: when the Todeket Ghost is seen, someone dies. And that in turn proves that if the ghost is real, then life exists after death. That means Jacob lives on somewhere, in Heaven."

"Geneve murdering Kynaston would prove nothing."

"To us, yes. To a madwoman—I'm not so sure."

Sequoia paced, walking three steps before turning again, constrained by the room's dimensions. "I don't believe it."

"You overestimate their morals because they're your kin," said Mattie. "I've always sensed, deep in the deepest part of my heart, that I was born into wealth and privilege. I have memories of grand houses and women in beautiful gowns. Yet I'm without any knowledge of my parents. The orphanage refused to tell me anything—I think because they were trying to protect me. It's only since coming here to Todeket that I've learned of my true heritage."

Her eyes stared into some distant space where shadow puppets played against the wall. "There's no doubt I'm related to the woman in the portrait. You saw it yourself. And this past year, as I've learned the story of the Desole widow and what your grandfather did during the war, I've realized the truth: I am the heir of a grand and noble family, nearly exterminated by injustice. A family which it is my duty to restore."

Sequoia looked at her. "Is that what this is about for you? Settling old debts?"

"I have no interest in vengeance," she said. "The past is gone. What worries me more is the future. Had it not been for the Wescotts' depredations, I would have an inheritance. Instead what does my family have to show for the war? The Desole seat burned to ashes and our womenfolk murdered."

"There isn't a person in America who wasn't affected by the war. You're not special. Your complaint is with the nature of war itself."

"Is it? And yet tonight and for many nights your uncle sat in his summer home beneath a stolen painting of *my* ancestress, crowing about what good fortune the war brought him. You heard him yourself: he owes all his success in business to the war. His business involves ruining other people, destroying them, running them into the gutter."

"I've read the newspaper stories." Doubt entered Sequoia's voice.

"Then you understand his infamy derives from the war. His own father was a murderer. His remaining son is a beast who shackles his wife to his tempers and drunkenness. I didn't know Jacob, but—"

"The failings of others aren't proof Geneve is a murderess."

"This family is evil. It sprouted from evil and its only

fruit is others' misery. Yesterday predicts the morrow."

Sequoia pinched an empty ampoule between thumb and forefinger. "But you had the means."

"I keep my bag in the sitting room off Geneve's bedroom. Anyone could walk in and grab the Cure, as much as they wanted."

She regarded Sequoia carefully as she said this, gauging his reaction, and when he said nothing, she stood and crossed the short distance to stand before him. There was nowhere to go where she wouldn't be close to him.

"My wife," he began, his voice rough, his throat tight. "Her name was Anna. I know what it's like to lose family. My parents are dead, my sisters moved so far west I'll likely never see them again."

"You had children?"

He didn't answer right away. "No."

Mattie laid her hand on his arm. "You have my greatest condolences."

"I am unlucky. Cursed." Sequoia shook his head and something inside rattled loose. "Ever since I was a child I've been susceptible to deep glooms and introversions. So much so that I wanted to end my life. I've tried several times, or at least started to. But I'm too unlucky for success, even of that kind."

He looked at her, apprising her reaction. She waited for him to continue.

"I know my despondency for what it is. It's like I stand outside myself and see my despair covering me, inhabiting me, yet I cannot take any step to lift it. But then it breaks and I ascend, soaring into clear skies. I imagine it God's consolation for the pitch darkness that comes before."

"You don't have to suffer," said Mattie. "These moods can be assuaged. There are chemicals."

"It doesn't matter. Injections can't offset the black cats and broken mirrors of the soul."

The tip of Mattie's pink tongue moistened her bottom lip. She stood very near.

"Your uncle has an account at the National City Bank—a large account," she said low. "Only two people are allowed to withdraw from it. Him, and your aunt. Geneve has been here on the island for the better part of the year. Your uncle brings cash to her when he visits, to maintain the house."

"Why are you telling me this?"

"Because Geneve is very sick and you are the only one who can help her. You already have a close relationship, more so than even I do after all these months. She can never leave the island again after what she's done tonight. She must be confined here. If you stayed, she would trust you to go to New York to run her errands. To shop and buy things she can't acquire around here. All the bank would need is a letter signed by Geneve authorizing you to make withdrawals for her. You would live comfortably and have the family you desire. You could be happy."

"And you?"

"I only want enough to begin the Desole line again, somewhere new. That's the faculty of women, to generate the family. We are as much spiritual mothers as physical."

History was a cipher, Sequoia told himself, a code for understanding the present. And yet there was no guarantee the translation was intelligible. Few argued the past didn't repeat itself, but when the newspaper was spread open and the day's affairs learned, it was never clear *which* past was reenacted before the reader. An event occurred and there were as many accounts of it as there were witnesses, each unique, yet still everyone assumed there was one true narrative, an absolute unshakeable lesson, to be applied forward.

All of the history books Sequoia read at sea were useless to him when he considered Mattie's words. One family saw itself as victor, its enemies the vanquished; the other saw itself as vindicators, their foes as plunderers. It was this, the inability to agree on a common chronicle, that rendered history meaningless, depreciating it from lesson and warning to pretext.

History for most was just an excuse, a rationalization to do what they'd already set their minds upon. Old prejudices thought dead and buried climbed with bony tenacity from their caskets, so determined to right bygone offenses, yet so blithely dismissive of repercussions. Sequoia understood some spiders devoured their mates as a matter of nature; and still the horror of that couldn't compare to the rationales of men who talked themselves into black deeds over some hoary grievance.

For a long moment Sequoia stared into Mattie's eyes and didn't fight what he saw there. But then his hands found themselves on her shoulders. Gently he pushed her away.

"I can't," he said. Just twelve hours ago, he could have. Just twenty-four hours ago, he most certainly would've. "Not to her."

Mattie regarded him through narrow eyes. "Her mind is gone, you know. It's nonsense what she believes about Jacob. Stealing from her would be like stealing an egg from a bird's nest—anger, and then forgetfulness. Because the rich can always lay another golden egg."

"No." He sat down on the bed to pull on his shoes. "I won't tell them what you've told me. But leave Geneve out of this."

"I can't take that risk."

She stabbed Sequoia in the neck, a syringe clutched in her fist. Almost immediately she stepped backward out of reach.

He stared up at her as he pulled the syringe from his artery.

"The Cure works much faster when injected directly into the bloodstream," said Mattie. "With Mr. Kynaston it had to wind its way through his digestive system. But putting it in his drink was the only way."

Sequoia gaped at the empty syringe in his palm. Her words echoed strangely.

"Why him?" It was the only thing he could think of.

"To hurt them," she said. "To hurt them as they've hurt my family."

Sequoia stared past her. In the corner of the room, as if summoned by the mention of his name, stood John Kynaston.

"To avenge the name of Desole."

Sequoia didn't hear her, his vision focused on the silent figure only he could see, until the entire bedchamber slowly constricted and finally collapsed.

10

Sequoia woke, relieved to escape from sticky dreams half fantastical and half memory. Both were horrible to him.

Somewhere close, oars splashed. He felt the cool mistiness of a night breeze past his skin. Rope bound his wrists and ankles, connected to a line knotted around a large rock in the bottom of the boat.

He lay folded in the stern of the dinghy, looking up at Mr. Burke on the center thwart pulling the oars. Burke, seeing him awake, smiled, his teeth turmeric in the dim light of the hooded lantern sitting on the bottom boards. A ferryman and his charge, rowing across the Styx.

Sequoia blinked and shook his head trying to clear the cobwebs. A wave of nausea rose inside him and he lurched forward to spit over the side. Then he collapsed backward, lulled by the rocking motion.

"*Him the Almighty Power,*" said Burke, "*hurled headlong flaming from the ethereal sky/ with hideous ruin and combustion down/ to bottomless perdition, there to dwell.*" Each syllable enunciated perfectly. He laughed a loud whooping laugh, careless.

"You're not deaf," said Sequoia. It was Mrs. Burke who'd said that. A trick played upon him.

Burke laughed louder.

With a powerful pull of Burke's arms, the boat surged forward—then ground to a standstill. Burke dipped his oar tips again but they knocked against stone beneath the surface. The dinghy was stuck, the outgoing current breaking against its stern

Somewhere in the fog nearby the waves lapped against a rocky shore. They were somewhere close to the island but in the ebbing tide they'd struck a hidden shoal.

Burke, thinking this but a small delay in his errand of murder, shipped his oars. He stood to lean over the bow, his back to Sequoia, to push off the shoal with a gaff.

What the captain of the dinghy didn't know as he poked at the rock beneath them was that his passenger was a Jonah, doomed to deliver calamity to his shipmates; and whatever nereid or sea god he'd crossed now raised a webbed hand from the weedy bottom to stay his fate.

Sequoia rolled back, raised his legs, and with a kick that would have impressed a mule, landed both heels upon the other man's buttocks. Burke flipped nimbly over the gunwale head first, his skull striking against the shoal with a hollow knock, followed by a loud splash. Sequoia sat up and craned his neck over the side. Burke floated face-down in the water.

For a long moment Sequoia studied the body. He'd never killed a man before, or at least he'd never felt culpable in anyone's demise, and somewhere inside a voice suggested he should feel less numb about it than he did. Part of his inaction, no doubt, was attributable to the Keeley Cure still dribbling through his blood. But it was hard to feel too much empathy toward a man who anchored his feet to a stone before a midnight row, so neither apology nor prayer followed Burke into the water.

Burke hadn't floated far. With his bound hands, Sequoia reached overboard to snag the man's ankle hem to pull him closer. Then he awkwardly wrestled him into the boat, drenching himself in the process.

The rocking jimmied the boat free of the shoal and it began to drift with the current.

Sequoia contorted himself to wriggle the sailor's folding knife from his pocket. He pulled it open and pinned it between his knees to saw his wrists free. The line around his ankles followed.

In the fog Sequoia had no way of knowing where Todeket lay. His only strategy was to turn the boat and row against the outgoing current. Even someone who knew the waters well like Burke was mad to row into a night fog like the one around them. But presumably he hadn't intended to go far—only as far as some deep hole or pit offshore in which to drown Sequoia.

The oars dipped over and over, and doubt crept into him the longer he rowed. The Thimbles being numerous, he hoped for a light that would guide him to shore, either Todeket's or another's, then wait until either fog or night broke. But stopping to listen, he heard nothing beyond the drip of the water as it ran off the blades; and looking, he saw nothing except the walls around him, illuminated by the dim wick of the hooded lantern. He reset the oars and rowed onward.

A woman's laughter drifted toward him as if through multiple layers of gauze. Ahead clustered several globes of light. A house, he imagined, and he set his back into it.

Careful of running aground, he heard no waves as he approached. Yet the lights grew brighter and more numerous. He gave two hard pulls and turned in his seat, wondering if collision was imminent, when the bow of a large sailboat broke through the fog, and close-by, another one, and the stern of a third.

A voice from one of them called out. "Looks like someone's late to the social. Ahoy."

Before him a flotilla of sailboats rode at anchor, lying very close together with bumpers between them. Lanterns hung from shrouds or sat upon decks, and among them Sequoia guessed nearly a dozen people watched his approach, drinks in hand.

Sequoia called up to them. "Can you tell me which way Todeket Island is?"

At the mention of Todeket several of the men looked at each other and a few of the women giggled.

"Todeket?" said a man. "Never heard of it." He smiled as he spoke, and Sequoia wasn't sure if he was joking.

"Please, it's important. I have a man here—he's injured. He needs attention."

The diluted lamplight magnified the ghastliness of the purplish mark on Burke's forehead. The speaker's face grew more serious. "Bring him aboard. We have a few doctors here."

Sequoia maneuvered to the boat's aft quarter, where the man threw him a line. The boats lay so close together that people could easily step from one to another, and a few more men appeared to help lift Burke from the rowboat. They murmured among themselves, and, with Burke's arms over their shoulders, carried him off, disappearing into the mist.

Sequoia accepted the grip of the man who first addressed him and stepped over the rail onto the sailboat. "Will he be all right, do you think?"

"Hard to say," said the man. "He's alive but that's a bad bump on his head. Some of the others will take him to shore. Shame to see Burke in such a state."

"You know him."

"Burke? Of course. He's a fixture on Todeket. His father built the house there."

Sequoia said, "You must be the Knickerbockers—the yacht club from New York."

"As you say." He offered his hand. "Benjamin Haywood."

"Sequoia Owen." They shook.

The two sat alone on the sailboat. In the cockpits of the others nearby sat mixed groups in summertime party clothes, chattering among themselves. They ignored Sequoia yet several times he caught a few of the women regarding him, almost in appraisal.

"Won't you stay for a drink?" asked Haywood. "I'm not entirely sure which direction Todeket is." He waved his hand. "Somewhere over there, I think."

A great sandbag of exhaustion fell on Sequoia's shoulders. He still felt a little lightheaded from the morphine and he felt no rush to return. "A drink would be very kind right now."

Haywood smiled and turned around, and when he turned back, offered Sequoia a glass of gin. Sequoia drank it in nearly one gulp.

"Haywood," said Sequoia. "I feel like I know that name from somewhere. Are you familiar with Mr. and Mrs. Tracy? They're Knickerbockers too."

"I think I've met them, yes." Something in Haywood's eyes suggested no recognition of the name. "But I don't know every member of the club. I can't imagine you've read my name in a newspaper. I'm not famous for anything."

"Maybe that wasn't it. Perhaps it was your Christian name. My wife—I had the strangest dream just now."

"The only way to sleep in this abominable heat is with a few more of these." Haywood rattled his glass.

Sequoia rubbed his temples. No point in trying to explain what led him to that moment. Like anything in a life, none of it made sense to anyone not living it.

"My wife, Anna," said Sequoia, "she became very

religious. When we married she was a churchgoer but not overly earnest. That changed. I was at sea for long periods. I think her faith sustained her during my absences."

"Faith is a buoy that can never be sunk. A fine use of her time."

Sequoia regarded him. "It's funny that you say that word—*use*. It was in my dream."

They had been seated at the kitchen table. "God loves harmony and precision," Anna said to him. That part happened, Sequoia felt sure.

But what she said afterward was a jumble, a mix of things Anna may have believed but never said, confused with the sentiments of Swedenborg.

"That is why he has created this system of pure order—so that every soul knows where he or she stands, and what they must do to better themselves and thereby strive to be closer to him. It's like being promoted at some employment on Earth. Only instead of better wages, here you may earn nearness to his perfection."

"Advancement in every employment I ever held," said the dream Sequoia to the dream Anna, "was less about the labor and more about flattering and kowtowing to the whims of those officers directly above me."

"My analogy may be imperfect but I'm sure you understand the point."

"On the contrary, I suspect you're spot on. Success after death is probably less about pleasing God and more about pleasing his bureaucrats. Just as in life."

"I'm teaching you how to succeed. How to find your use."

"*Use* sounds an awful lot like *work*," said Sequoia.

None of that had ever transpired, and yet so much of it sounded like something Anna *would've* said.

"You speak of your wife in the past tense," said Haywood, sitting with him in the boat. "You have my condolences."

For a brief second that terrible moment flashed before him again, when he expected to arrive and see Anna holding their baby. Instead: his descent down the gangplank, bag slung over his shoulder, searching the crowd on the quay, only to see his father standing side-by-side with Anna's sister, veiled and dressed in black. And then, when he'd shoved his way through to him, his father's words, the first words said to him by any family in months: *There was a complication.*

"Thank you," said Sequoia to Haywood. He remembered now: Benjamin. Before he'd embarked that final time, they talked about what to name the baby. They agreed on Benjamin, if a boy.

Suddenly Sequoia wanted to be away from there, from that strange muted party at sea, the voices of the partygoers muffled and the lamplight dulled by fog. A continuation of his delusion, and it made him sick.

"You said something just now," said Sequoia, "about Burke. About his father building the house."

"I did say something about that, yes. The Burkes are old-time residents of the area. I think the younger more or less inherited his father's position. They kept the senior Burke on for a long while at the house, until he died."

"When was that?"

"Oh, about eight years ago, during the Russian flu. Died in his bed."

"Upon the island."

"Yes. He'd been decrepit for a while and more or less unable to work. It was very nice of the Wescotts to keep him on, I think."

Sequoia said, "You know a lot about Todeket."

"I've been on these waters for years." Haywood's face was completely neutral.

Sequoia heard laughter, and looked over to see several children scampering across the deck of one of the boats. They quickly vanished into the cabin.

"Tell me about the house," Sequoia said. "The older Burke built it and then sold it to the Wescotts?"

"No. The older Burke built it under the direction of Isaiah Wescott, who'd bought the island. Wescott had a very specific plan for the house, and he hired Burke to build it."

Haywood leaned forward. "Here's a funny thing you may not know. To cut costs, Burke actually used parts of other buildings in the construction. Foreclosures sold off at auction by the sheriff, that sort of thing. I think a number of the windows came from a bank that caught fire, leaving only them and the brick walls intact. Even a few desacralized churches in there."

"That accounts for the hodgepodge style of the house."

"That was all Wescott. Most of the reused parts were buried under the façade or trim work. A coat of paint here or some shingles there and you'd never know that two adjoining walls had been lifted from separate houses."

"I've heard so many stories about the house, I don't know what to believe."

"All fiction, I suspect," said Haywood. "But the most convincing lie is the one that's closest to the truth. We tell them to each other and we choose to believe them for our own reasons. It's a shame you can't ask Burke—*your* Mr. Burke. He knows the nature of that house better than anyone."

A feeling of euphoria had overtaken Sequoia as he traveled north from Virginia to Connecticut. He believed at long last, after a string of misfortune, events would be decided one way or another in his life: either he would be embraced by the Wescotts and discover his future with them; or he would be cast out penniless, his last gambit misplayed, onto the streets without a single friend. In his mind's eye he saw himself strolling down Park Avenue, nodding and dipping his top hat to passersby, pausing only to toss a nickel into the frostbitten hands of a man squatting over a steaming grate—a man who, remarkably, bore the same face as Sequoia. These two possibilities existed side-by-side in his imagination, and it was this emotion, an all-or-nothing elation, that ticked upward in his soul as the train crossed each minute and second of latitude.

It had only been yesterday. Or the day before, he wasn't sure.

"I should get back," said Sequoia. He set down his empty glass. "Tell the family what's happened to him."

"You're sure you won't stay and have another? I feel badly setting you loose in this fog."

"No, I better not." He very much wanted to be away.

Haywood did not look pleased. "Can't be helped, then."

Sequoia returned to his rowboat and threw Haywood the line.

"Row in that direction." Haywood pointed as Sequoia shoved away. "Todeket lies on the eastern edge of the Thimbles. At night, Mrs. Burke lights a pair of lanterns in the topmost windows of the house to guide sailors. The *deux soleils*, they're called—the two suns. Look for them."

Sequoia dipped his oars and rowed, his back toward his goal, his face toward the flotilla. Haywood stood watching him with a frown. And then the voices dimmed into silence and the lamps faded, and the Knickerbockers dissipated in the fog like a page wiped with a rubber eraser.

11

The boat and its rower bobbed through the vapor like a glass fishing float, a globe of life and motion in the deadening mist. Sequoia doubted Haywood's directions, even if he couldn't think of any rationale for Haywood to mislead him. But finally he heard a crash of wave on stone and, looking over his shoulder, saw a pair of watery lights staring at him from just above the treetops. A pair of lamps, set on the sills of the two eyebrow windows in the upper roof of the house.

Suddenly a door inside him unlocked. This same scene had played itself once before—he remembered now, coming to the island as a child, the ferryman bringing him and his mother to the island at night. His sister Patty had been there too, just a baby, but not the youngest, Mary, who wouldn't have been born yet. Was it the same trip as the lunch at the St. Nicholas?

Distinctly Sequoia remembered the approach, spotting the two lights—the two suns, Haywood called them—through a thin veil of mist. The trees weren't as tall, and he recalled a gloomy figure standing on the dock with a lantern. Waiting.

Other images sprang up too. A grim-faced man with wild, uncombed white hair, sitting in a chair in the parlor with blankets over his legs, and Sequoia being commanded by—who? his mother?—to go over and shake his hand. Looking up the nighttime stairs and refusing to climb them, overcome by terrible dread of the darkness above. Being turned out into the yard on a hot day so the grown-ups could talk, wandering aimlessly between the island's pines.

Brief, almost static memories, disjointed and inexplicable. If his sister was an infant, Sequoia couldn't have been much more than three or four. Had their mother brought her children to the island to meet their grandfather, a visit never repeated and, as far as he could recall, never mentioned upon their return to Virginia?

There was no one left to ask about it. His mother was dead, his grandfather too, his sisters gone west and out of reach except by letter or telegram. Sequoia had no recollection of his uncle on the island, so even Preston might not know; perhaps he and his family remained in New York while Sequoia's mother went farther north.

Just another mystery, another memory or story dredged from the mud, for which no suitable answer or explanation would ever be provided. His mother cut herself off from her kin to follow her husband into a strange land, and their children grew to adulthood knowing almost nothing of a whole half of their genealogical tree—for this, Sequoia would never receive an account. His father ruined himself in Connecticut over a passion so fleeting its adherents would spend the rest of their lives trying to explain it. That would also go forever unclarified.

Sequoia bumped the rowboat against the dock and leapt out with the lamp, not even bothering to tie up. Let the tide take it.

He avoided the path, instead hooking left through the trees to approach the kitchen door indirectly. The gravel and pine needles and fallen sticks ground into his bare feet. Their limbs pushed and swiped against him, jealous of what they protected.

Sequoia thrust through the last of them and immediately stumbled over a pile of stones. Around him the cairns of the island graveyard rose out of the night, the light of the lamp shining on their slick humps.

Onward the lean-to chapel appeared, and from there he caught and followed the trail to the house. The wet grass and slapping branches soaked the lower legs of his trousers by the time he reached the door.

Beyond the black and uninhabited kitchen, a light dimly glowed from the parlor.

"Good lord," said his uncle when he saw him, "you look a mess. Where are your shoes?"

And in fact Sequoia was a mess: in shirtsleeves without coat or cravat; his trousers wet around the calves; his feet sandy. He collapsed into a chair across from Preston.

"Forgive me," he said, "but I've endured no fewer than three attempts on my life since sundown. I'm afraid my appearance has suffered for it."

Preston squinted at him but said nothing, too incurious by nature to ask what he meant. Beside them, still beneath the tablecloth, lay John Kynaston. A few candles flickered around the room.

"Keeping vigil, I see," said Sequoia.

For a long moment, Preston didn't respond. Then he said, "Have you ever heard the story of Farragut when we sailed up the Mississippi past the forts?"

"No."

Preston readjusted himself in his seat. "There were two forts. On the south bank of the Mississippi River was Fort Jackson and on the north bank was Fort St. Philip—this was during the capture of New Orleans in sixty-two. We'd previously taken the mouth of the river but the two forts sat almost across from each other at a bend in the river. They were the only thing stopping the Union from retaking New Orleans, which at the time was the Confederacy's biggest port. The difficulty lay in the fact that there was no way to maneuver into range of the forts without ourselves being caught in their crossfire. Between them, they had almost two hundred guns. It was an impossible task.

"But Admiral Farragut recognized that New Orleans was the goal, not the forts. He believed it was the army's job to capture the forts from behind, just as Benjamin Arnold did at Groton and New London. All Farragut had to do was make it past the forts and then seize New Orleans. This would cut off the forts from any relief or supplies and make them easier to capture.

"And that's what we did. The artillery softened up the forts with some mortars and then at three o'clock on the morning of April 24, we sailed north along the river in two columns. John and I were onboard the USS *Brooklyn*, in the second column behind Farragut's flagship. The Grays had set up a chain in the river strung between buoys with a gap in the middle, and just as the first column passed through it, they spotted us and opened their cannons. We obliged them likewise, none of us slowing a single knot. It was a race to make it past the forts as quickly as possible and out of the range of their guns.

"The sky that night went from pitch black to the Fourth of July, shells arcing overhead if they overshot or sending up geysers if they fell short, or sometimes crashing through the decks and rigging. It wasn't just the forts either—the Grays had their ships too, waiting upriver. They had an ironclad, the *Manassas*, which rammed the *Mississippi* in the first column, and then when she didn't sink, came downriver and rammed us. We declined to sink as well. Farragut's ship dodged a fire raft and stuck in the shallows, although they managed to free themselves and rejoin the action.

"You possess the luxury of knowing how the story ended: we lost one vessel, the Rebels lost twelve. New Orleans was returned to Federal control, and the army did in fact capture the forts from land. But at the time, there were no prophets among us. I don't mind telling you that I was more afraid beforehand than during the battle. Thinking about what we had to do, the anticipation of it, was the worst part. Once it started, everything happened so fast I think if I'd died I wouldn't have noticed at all. I imagine I would have been at my post, perhaps heard the whine of the shell, and then known nothing but utter annihilation. That's how I wish death to be. Sudden darkness."

"That is not the wish of a spiritualist."

"No. I suppose not."

"But you remember your friend John," Sequoia said, "and so he lives on, in a fashion. Your father served in the war, was wounded. He's not forgotten."

Preston snorted. "If you only knew the truth."

"What truth is that?"

Preston leaned forward. "My father wasn't wounded in the war. Or at least, not wounded by someone else."

Sequoia digested this, his uncle watching him carefully.

Preston tapped his finger against his head. "My father shot himself. The whole story about the house in the swamp? The old woman? Made up. A complete falsehood. The whole thing was concocted by that sergeant who served under him—Barber or Bauer, I don't remember which. Incredibly loyal. He did it to preserve my father's honor."

Sequoia shook my head. "But there were other men, other marines. He couldn't have. They would've known what really happened."

"Oh, maybe the bones of the story are true, about a

house in a swamp somewhere. But he did it, all right—
he shot himself and survived. The sergeant wove it so
that he'd been shot by the enemy instead. The doctors
who treated him deduced the reality but they went
along and discharged my father, just to keep the whole
thing quiet."

"What about the portrait in the dining room?"

Preston shrugged. "I have no idea where that came
from—maybe they did take it from some decayed
mansion. Who knows. The point is, Isaiah Wescott had
an infection, a hereditary melancholy, and it's seeped
through the generations like a jar of molasses spilled
at the top of a staircase. This whole family is gripped
by an inescapable madness going all the way back to
your grandfather, if not beyond. And Jacob finally suc-
cumbed to it."

Sequoia heard a riddle once, while standing at the
rail of an uneventful dog watch, in which it was theo-
rized that he'd arrived at a pair of gates, each guarded
by a sentinel, one of whom always told the truth and
one who always spoke lies. To determine which gate
led to his destination, he was allowed to ask one of the
guards a single question. What, then, to ask?

For Sequoia, solving the puzzle interested him less
than the scenario itself, which portrayed two men otherwise indistinguishable save for their esteem or antipathy for truth. This seemed to metaphorize all mankind.

Perhaps *all* of it was true—the house in the swamp,
the old woman, and the mysterious shadows and

dreams; but also the stories about the smallpox graves and the ruined Desoles and a house stitched together from other buildings. Everything and nothing could be believed. Truth was a hotel buffet where every diner ladled different foods atop his plate, in different amounts, and no two departed the table having eaten the same meal.

"You say Jacob suffered from melancholy," said Sequoia. "Then why not grant him permission to marry the girl he loved? If the two of them were happy together, why not extend to him a reprieve from his distress?"

"Because I'm his father and I knew better."

"Life is so tenuous, as you mentioned. So full of anguish. We spend half our time asleep and countless hours too sick or exhausted or busy earning our wages to enjoy it. I mean, if only for the sake of granting Jacob one moment of happiness you could've set aside your decorum and given peace to your son."

"What you suggest," said Preston, "is that by denying him my blessing, I made Jacob pull the trigger of the weapon. You assign me a culpability I don't accept. Jacob didn't *have* to kill himself—he chose to do it. He wasn't locked in a room, with the only exit through a gun barrel. There are a hundred, a thousand more girls who could've been his wife. Instead he made up his mind that either Rachel should be his or he would extinguish himself. It was childish."

"You don't regret your obstruction."

"If I have one regret, it's that I didn't instill in Jacob the fortitude to withstand the disappointments of living."

There was, deep inside Sequoia, a flicker of anger that wanted to rise into a flame. Exhaustion dampened it. What sat before him was not some threatening villain or ruthless tyrant, running his enemies to ground in the gutter of Wall Street, but instead an old man who fabricated the walls of his life so tall that only noontime sunshine could fall within. No shadows lay across his tread, no darkness lurked in the corners, because he kept the rooms of his mind swept clean and unfurnished.

Just as Preston saw only the benefit of war, likewise he saw only the blessings of life. And when, by some chance, an evil happened to drop into his existence, one too enormous to ignore—like the death of his greatest friend or even that of his own son—it rattled his bones because it reminded him of something he'd rather pretend didn't exist. But Sequoia knew this black mood of Preston's would fade the moment Kynaston's body left his sight. His uncle would lock the memory of tonight inside a locker, then shove it with a kick under the bed to remain forgotten and unseen.

Footsteps sounded behind Sequoia from the doorway. "Clearly I'm not the only who can't sleep. Good lord," said Andrew when he saw Sequoia, "what happened to you?"

"I'm happy to report that I escaped Mr. Burke's attempt to drown me—at your instruction."

"My instruction? Whatever are you babbling about?" Andrew went to a sideboard and poured himself a whiskey, then pulled over a chair and sat. "I heard a commotion upstairs and found Mattie in your bedroom. You were slumped in the corner. She said you'd suffered a fit and that she'd given you morphine to calm you. We didn't know what to do with you so Burke and I carried you downstairs to the dock and I ordered him to row you to a doctor on the mainland." He gulped his drink. "Now you're back again. Damn nuisance."

Sequoia sat up in his chair. He almost believed him: Andrew's irritation was too sincere to be an act. "You didn't tell Burke to drown me?"

Andrew glanced at his father. "Is he insane or just stupid?" Then to Sequoia, "Why on earth would he *drown* you? He was taking you to shore."

It wasn't Andrew who tried to strangle him during the séance.

"Burke's father died on the island. Haywood said that." Sequoia leapt up, went over to the bookshelf to seize the album.

"What is he on about?" Andrew asked.

Sequoia turned to the page—the page listing the deaths on the island.

9 Jul. 1868. Jer. Wescott. Drowned.

6 June, 1872. Pearl Wescott. Drowned.
August 23, 1874. Benj. Hayward. Drowned.
Aug. 9, 1883. Gretch. Phelps Wescott. Drowned.
May 25, 1884. Esthr. Watkins. Fall.
July 26 1885. Isaiah Wescott. Infirmity.
Sep 4, 1887. Silas Burbidge. Drowned.
3/25/90. L. Burke. Influenza.
8/9/97. J. Wescott. Accident.

He tapped the page.

"Jacob was the last person to die on the island," Sequoia said. "Geneve said something. She said, *I fear the ghost and Jacob are one and the same.* But why would she say that when legends of ghosts go back thirty years, to the very beginning of the house?"

The other two men stared at him.

Sequoia pointed at the book. "Why is it that so many people died on the island but there's only a *single* ghost? If ghosts exist, then this house should be wall-to-wall wraiths and specters. I mean, on the average someone drops dead here every three years."

He flipped to the pages about the Todeket Ghost. "Some say the ghost is a man, others say it's a woman. But they all agree there's only one of them. They never see multiple ghosts at a time." Then to Preston, he said, "There's something you're not telling me about the legend. I think you know it. And I know Geneve does. Something she believes."

"I have no idea what's happening right now," said

Andrew, "but *I* believe you're very agitated and another shot of morphine is called for. I'll get Mattie."

But as he stood, Preston said, "Sit down, Andrew," and he produced a pistol from the pocket of his dressing gown. He pointed the barrel at Sequoia.

Sequoia noticed that one of the dueling pistols from the wall between the windows was absent. Cap-lock, muzzle loading. Capable of firing a single shot.

"Father," said Andrew, "what are you doing?"

"I'm protecting our family," he said.

Paper dolls, thought Sequoia.

"Is that it?" Sequoia asked. "Or are you performing one last favor for John Kynaston—the newest Todeket Ghost."

Andrew reached for the pistol but Preston evaded his grasp. "Put that thing down immediately," Andrew said. "It's not even loaded."

"To the contrary," said Preston. "I keep it loaded for just such an occasion as this."

"On what occasion would you need a loaded pistol on a private island?"

But his father ignored him. "Geneve worked it out too," he said to Sequoia. "Whether there's any truth to it doesn't matter. As you say, it's what she *believes*. And she believed Jacob was trapped in this house. Imprisoned. Prevented from being with our Lord."

Sequoia put down the commonplace book and stood straight, fists at his side. Every nerve tighter than a backstay.

"But now Jacob is free," said Sequoia. "Because Kynaston died here tonight. Instead of me. That's how it works. It's a game of hot potato."

"I don't —" Preston licked his lips. "That's not why I'm doing this."

"Why did Jacob really kill himself?" Sequoia asked. "What happened to the girl, Rachel? Where is she now?"

Across the room the reels of the Mechanical Oracle spun wildly.

The noise shocked everyone. The pistol cracked, the shot zipping past Sequoia's ear as he lunged for the floor.

Behind him wood and plaster splintered.

"Of all the cruelest luck," said Preston, regarding the smoking pistol in his hand, "for the target to be so close and the bullet still miss its mark."

12

Sequoia slept until almost noon. He woke to a breeze whistling through the open window, carrying with it the cry of gulls and the pounding of waves. Though still dense with summer humidity, the air was offset by the coolness of morning. For a brief ephemeral moment he felt like a child again, lying in his bed at home, the very first emotion in his breast an excitement for the day ahead. He blinked and it passed, but for at least an hour afterward he remained amazed he could still feel it at all.

As he dressed he noticed a sheet of paper lying on the floor, slipped under the door while he slept.

Do not concern yourself with me Friend. As you say my wait shll Not be Long. The blockaid of a port Demands patients. *—JK*

More nonsense. Sequoia crumpled the paper into a ball and tossed it into a corner.

He finished dressing and drifted into the kitchen with the intent of making himself a cup of coffee before summoning a ferry back to town. Instead Mrs. Burke waved him out of her way and ordered him to sit. Minutes later, she set not only a mug in front of him but also a plate with three fried eggs, four rashers of bacon, and a slice of toast.

It amazed Sequoia even more when Mrs. Burke sat down across from him with a cup of her own, and kept up a steady stream of chatter while he ate.

Much had transpired while Sequoia lay abed. The police had been summoned, and together with his uncle Preston, they removed the body of John Kynaston to the mainland, where Preston remained to answer questions and, more tragically, deliver the news to the man's widow, present somewhere among the islands or Knickerbocker yachts.

Sequoia felt some regret; he wished to say goodbye to his uncle before departing. Preston was still his mother's brother.

The other bit of news concerned Mattie's departure. She had quit the house not long before Sequoia's arrival in the kitchen, but Mrs. Burke could not say if she had resigned her post or been dismissed. Certainly the mistress of the house was feeling better and no longer had any need of a nurse. His aunt already told the others about returning to New York.

As she droned on, Mrs. Burke fidgeted with her coffee cup, spinning it in slow circles on the tabletop without ever lifting it to her lips. Sequoia surmised there was something she either wanted from him, or some favor she begged to ask, but she was so unaccustomed to simple human niceties that she possessed little knowledge of how to go about it.

Sequoia still had one question about the island; and suddenly he saw a way it might be answered.

"What a fine day it is," he said, staring beyond the glass at the sunlight on the pines. "A good day to be on the Sound. By the way, is Mr. Burke around? I thought he might row me to shore later."

"I haven't seen Mr. Burke all morning," Mrs. Burke said. The subject broached, floodwaters poured forth. "I don't know where that husband of mine has run off to. His shed is empty and the dinghy is gone but usually he informs me before going to town. Too much labor involved to row there on his own, only to return and have me send him back on some errand. Most days he goes about his business and I go about mine, but one rule we have is to discuss what's needed from shore before either of us goes there. Sometimes I take a ferry but he always rows, or we go together in the dinghy." She looked sharp at Sequoia. "You wouldn't happen to know where's he gone?"

He kept his attention on slicing and forking the runny eggs. "I haven't seen him."

"Strange." She spun the coffee cup, her gaze now toward the window. "He was already gone when I woke last night during the commotion, and he never came back to bed."

She referred to the discharge of the dueling pistol, which shook awake the entire house. The three men in the parlor, without discussion, agreed it was an accident.

Sequoia said, "You don't think something could've happened to him? That he could've been swept off last night?" An evil without legs coiled in the pit of his stomach and he almost shivered with the pleasure of it. "It would be a tragedy for someone with his condition to fall overboard—I mean, he'd be unable to cry out for help."

"He's not completely deaf, you know," she said. "People think he is. Just a little hard of hearing. This may surprise you, but he has a fine memory for poetry and recites it as well as William Gillette. You'd never know it about his ears, listening to him. Speaks the words crisp as biting into an apple."

"Is that so?"

"Oh, it's true. You should ask him when he gets back. He must've gone off on an errand. Now that's got me thinking." She tapped her fingertips against the cup. "Maybe Mr. Wescott asked him to row off and search the islands for Mrs. Kynaston? That must be it. He wouldn't have gone to town without telling me. He's out asking for Mrs. Kynaston, I'm sure. There isn't anything he wouldn't do for the master of the house, or its mistress—nothing either of us wouldn't do, really. We owe our livelihoods to the Wescotts. They're good people."

Sequoia mopped up the last of the yolk with the toast and pushed the empty plate aside. Without really looking at her, he asked, "Do you know if the girl Jacob was fond of ever came to the island? Rachel. Rachel Leeds."

Again Mrs. Burke squinted her eyes at Sequoia, a fox suspicious of a trap. "Now why would you ask that?"

His shoulders lifted in what he hoped wasn't too exaggerated of a shrug. "I've heard so much about her, I'm just curious to know how she got along with the family."

"Well." The coffee cup revolved another half-turn. "Jacob's parents liked her well enough. They just didn't approve of them marrying. She was *odd*, you know. Very much like Master Jacob. She did come here the one time, without being invited, last summer after Mr. and Mrs. Wescott forbade Jacob to propose to her. Said she wanted to see Jacob. Mr. Wescott and his sons were out sailing when she arrived, and Mrs. Wescott told her it was better that she leave and not come back. Very polite about it, she was, and civil—always civil. Said it was best if she didn't see Jacob. So Mr. Burke put her in the dinghy and the two of them rowed off. That was the last we saw of her. She never returned, as instructed. No one said a word about it to Jacob, either. A little secret to save him from further heartbreak."

"Mr. Burke's father died on the island some years before that? From the flu."

"What does that have to do with anything?"

"Nothing," said Sequoia. "Just something that sprang to mind." And he thanked Mrs. Burke for breakfast and left her to her gyrations.

On his way to the parlor to retrieve the Mechanical

Oracle he cut through the dining room. Nothing remained on the wall above Preston's seat of the mysterious girl and her flyswatter save a rectangle of slightly darker wallpaper. The heavy gold-painted frame of the portrait lay face-down on the table, the canvas absent. Of the two of them, at least Mattie Fuller got something she wanted.

Mrs. Burke's failure of housekeeping in the dining room extended to the parlor. The chairs stood everywhere, the drink glasses uncollected. The imprint of Kynaston's body still dented the sofa, and Sequoia wondered if the police, in their retrieval of the corpse, had made any awkward inquiries of his uncle regarding the bullet hole beside the door.

The Oracle sat exactly where he'd left it—after all, only now was it the most interesting thing in the room—and Sequoia replaced it in its container. Before he closed it shut, he glanced at the last advice given, the unasked-for prophecy that spun the wheels and spooked Preston into firing.

The danger is still certain, read the reels. *Your inheritance is ambiguous.*

Sequoia quickly snapped the latches and buckled the belt around the case.

As he crossed toward the door, a breath of air brushed against his cheek. The windows were open but it struck him as somehow strange, a wind blowing from the wrong quarter. It came from the bookshelf against the wall.

He set down the Oracle. The shelves were built-in, running floor to ceiling. But part of them, on his right, stood out from the rest by an eighth of an inch, creating a vertical seam. Carefully, he worked his fingertips along it, pulling it further, until an entire section swung away on silent hinges. A hidden door.

Beyond was a narrow shaft, perhaps two feet square, and a wooden ladder, leading down.

In the cellar, he blundered through screens of cobwebs and around brick columns and sticks of old furniture to a heavy wooden door. On a dusty stool lay a pair of black leather gloves.

Beyond the door, a steep and narrow stairwell brought him to the yard, just beside the kitchen door. The stack of firewood for the stove screened the cellar stairs from view.

"You'd do better to clean up after your handiwork," Sequoia said as he tossed the gloves at Lisette's feet. "Someone might unravel your tricks."

Lisette, unflappable in her laudanum calm, turned from her packing to regard the gloves lying on the bedroom floor.

"Whatever are those?" she asked.

"The gloves Burke wore when he tried to strangle me," said Sequoia. "He snuck into the room during the séance."

Lisette's eyes bore into him from under heavy lids. "And you believe I put Burke up to it? Why would I do that?"

"That was your plan—yours and Andrew's. If someone new died in the house, then Jacob's soul would be free. And Geneve could finally be at peace over his soul."

"You seem to have mixed your conspirators," Lisette said. "I suspected someone was trying to kill you. But why would you think I was the one behind it?"

"You tried to poison me."

Lisette chuckled. "Really, Mr. Owen, you're very suspicious. I assure you I did not. It was simply tea."

"Just like you didn't know Mattie wanted to steal from Geneve, I suppose." Sequoia's tone was less sure. "You hired her. She worked for you."

Chests and cases clogged every square inch of the chamber, and as she spoke, Lisette drifted from bureau to bed or closet to trunk, carrying some item for stowage. It reminded him of Mrs. Irving and her packages.

"It was the most serendipitous of events," she said. "When I went to the employment agency, they lined up the girls in front of me like a pageant. When I saw Mattie, I nearly fell out of my chair—it was the girl from the portrait, standing right before me. I brought her to Todeket and gave her a tour of the house. You should've seen her expression when I led her into the dining room to first lay eyes upon the painting.

"After that it was just a matter of suggestion. Tales about Carolina swamps and Isaiah during the war, bits and bobs of old family stories that I stretched and colored to her taste. Fairly soon I had Mattie Fuller the orphan believing she was Mattie Fuller, heir to a southern dynasty. What girl doesn't want to believe she's Cinderella?

"She came to me this morning and said her presence here was no longer tenable. That suited me just fine, so I paid her wages and sent her on her way. I even wrote her a letter of recommendation." Lisette indicated a roll-top desk against the wall.

"Mattie murdered Kynaston. She drugged his drink," said Sequoia. "She tried to drug me."

"There you go with your claims of poison again. What proof do you have?"

Beyond Mattie's own confession, he realized, none. He didn't even know where Kynaston's body was. "You wanted access to the account at National City Bank," he said.

"I may have suggested it to her. If she'd succeeded, all I needed to do was confront her. I would've happily accepted half in exchange for silence. Ah well—*c'est la vie*. But I had nothing to do with the séance. If you want to accuse anyone," she said, "you ought to accuse the biggest deceiver in this house."

Geneve was sitting up in bed, a dozen pillows propped behind her, the curtains half-drawn to allow the breeze but to keep the sun's heat in abeyance. She sat doing nothing, neither reading a book nor working at needlepoint or any other project. Her hands lay next to her on the sheets, her palms turned upward, and as Sequoia entered and pulled up a chair beside the bed, it struck him that she seemed to be simply bathing in a kind of ineffable joy.

She beamed at him. "Mrs. Burke told me that you intend to leave. You're welcome to stay, Sequoia. As long as you like."

"The house is too strange for me," he said.

"But that will pass. The shadow," said Geneve, "has been *lifted*. No more falsehoods. No more worry over Jacob." She wagged her finger at him. "Never discount a mother's intuition."

Sequoia said, "But is it really that much of a relief when a man died here last night?"

Geneve stared toward the end of the bed, out the window. For a moment she didn't answer. Then she said, "Swedenborg teaches that we must live by the truth, for God adores truth, and therefore we must accept it no matter where it leads us. And frankly," she said, "even if the legend isn't true, it assuages my soul to *believe* Jacob is now free of this place. Free to move on."

Sequoia knew many people who never truly recovered from the death of someone close. Forever after they cringed at the pronunciation of a loved one's name, its syllables transformed from love song to dirge. Perhaps a blithe attitude was the better mindset; perhaps the elevation of a few blessings reduced the weight of tragedy's chains. Even optimists will admit a cosmos filled with at least as much bad as good— otherwise there wouldn't be a need for their ideology.

Maybe there was a lesson for Sequoia there, if he chose to submit to the tutor.

After all, as far as the Wescotts knew, Kynaston died of natural causes.

Yet twice, at least, Burke attempted to kill Sequoia. That wasn't natural. Sequoia could not imagine his reasoning for acting alone. He assumed Andrew culpable, maybe Lisette too, motivated by a sincere desire to soothe his mother's worry. Judging from Geneve's improved condition, the logic was sound. But Lisette denied involvement and even Andrew himself seemed ignorant. Both struck him as sincere. Likewise Preston's actions the night before presented themselves as rash and irrational, borne of anguish, and doomed to failure—for it was the sensible and self-possessed who was least likely to succeed in affairs of passion.

That left only a last possibility.

As he sat there beside his aunt, the thoughts flashing electrically through his mind, his old habit of sometimes speaking what he pondered resurfaced, and without meaning to, very low, in almost a whisper, Sequoia said, "What did you tell Burke to do?"

But Geneve, misunderstanding, appraised him with a critical gaze, assessing perhaps what to say and what not to. "Don't think too poorly of me for my little subterfuge. The girl came here last summer to see Jacob. I sent her away, and I told Mr. Burke to be certain she didn't return. He took my instructions a little too faithfully, I think. But I can't say I'm sorry. Jacob found out later. There were letters—someone sent him letters, telling him. We found them all over his room. I burned them, of course, every last one."

She reached out and gripped Sequoia's arm. "I needed a friend, someone to believe me. You *are* that friend. God sent you to Todeket for that reason—you are the agent of his mercy. That is your use. I'm not sorry what I did. What I told Mr. Burke to do, last summer or last night. But you survived and John died instead. So all is well."

Geneve opened a drawer in the nightstand beside her. "You have my thanks. I recognize one cannot pay the landlord or the oyster house in words." From the drawer she took a folded check, which she handed to him. "A gift given in gratitude."

Sequoia could tell he was expected to unfold the check and read the amount, so he did. He swallowed unconsciously. Spent judiciously, it would support him for more than a year. Long enough, at least, to see if the Mechanical Oracle was worth anything to the American public.

He looked at her and she looked back at him. In her regard there lay a certain despotism, a tyranny demanding that he say or do nothing in protest, for the gift so easily dispensed could just as easily be rescinded. There could be no equivocation, nothing less than an unquestioning acceptance of it, or she would turn on him. But likewise there was something of the beggar in that expression too, an asking for alms. It was a request to accept the ostensible, to acknowledge that the truth of Jacob and her and everything Wescott extended no deeper than a finger-length beneath the surface. She herself knew her peace was extremely tenuous, a kingdom built upon lake ice in early spring. A crack from him and it would collapse.

His hands wanted to rip the check into halves but they trembled too much. "Thank you," said Sequoia, and for the rest of his life he would never know if it was spoken out of greed for himself or pity for her. "I cannot—" He trailed off, feeling a little sick staring at the paper. A pair of pennies taken from his own sockets, the fare paid to the boatman.

"Goodbye." He left it at that.

The day was blindingly bright, the sky a lapis blue punctuated by an occasional cotton-spun cloud. The light made Sequoia slightly nauseous. He would've shielded his eyes had his hands been free, but by the time he reached the dock his squint adapted. He set down his bag and the Oracle's case, and from a protective sleeve he unfurled the red flag and hooked its grommets on the pegs of a piling. A sturdy bench sat at the foot of the dock, and Sequoia sat and waited for a ferryman to respond.

Andrew emerged from the cabin of the sailboat tied to the dock. Neither acknowledged the other, at least not immediately. "You know," said Andrew finally, "the first time I had my portrait taken—just by myself as a young man, without the family—I saw the photograph and didn't recognize it." As he spoke, he moved about the deck, removing the covers for the main and jib sails, making ready to get underway. "I thought to myself, *Do I really look like this?* It's because we only see ourselves in the mirror. From that singular angle alone. When we see ourselves from a different perspective, it confounds us."

Sequoia thought of the check in his pocket and said, "I think each of us is seeing himself in a clearer light today."

"What are you talking about?" said Andrew. "I'm speaking of my mother. I wanted her to make peace with Jacob. All of us understood his reasons for doing it, even if those reasons were foolish to us. Jacob was peculiar, with peculiar ideas. I could accept that. My mother could not. She sees herself from the one direction and I see her from another." He pointed at the bow line. "Here, untie the painter."

As Sequoia undid the line, Andrew stepped onto the dock and unspooled the stern line from the cleat, then hopped nimbly back onboard again. When Sequoia had thrown him the bow line, Andrew said, "Push me off."

Sequoia planted his sole against the bow and shoved the boat away from the dock.

"It's like the market, really," said Andrew. "It's less about fighting the madness of the mob and more about being first to sell them torches and pitchforks. One must be practical even in the face of lunacy." As the sailboat backed into the deeper water, Andrew adjusted the tiller, then eased the boom slightly and leapt to raise the main sail. A gust of wind caught the canvas and the boat began to creep forward. Sequoia confessed to himself the maneuver was expertly done.

"In my opinion," said Sequoia, loud so that Andrew could hear, "your mother is even more relentless and cold-blooded in regard to family than you are in business."

"Of course she is," said Andrew. "My mother is a Wescott and all Wescotts believe the same thing—a man who cannot tolerate small misfortunes will never accomplish great things. But you're not a Wescott, as much as you may like to be. That's why it's not worth the bother talking to you." And with that, the boom sprang out and the sail bulged with wind. The boat jumped toward the Sound and was soon out of earshot.

Sequoia followed in slow pursuit, accompanying the sailboat's course by pacing along the granite slabs of the shoreline, hand cupped over his eyes. Andrew piloted the boat down the channel past Exton's Reef, then tacked south. Behind him, Sequoia heard the putter of a steam launch, and he turned to see a ferryman heading toward the vacant dock in response to the flag. The ferryman waved and Sequoia waved back.

He cast a last glance at the sailboat's stern. From there Sequoia could see the length of Todeket's western shore, with its worn coast of smoothened rock and, farther from the water, its curtain of pitch pines. Just as he was about to turn, he noticed a figure standing inside the trees, likewise watching the sailboat recede into the glittering horizon. Sequoia couldn't make out who it was, although the figure's silhouette was very round at the belt. As if aware of his scrutiny, the other swiveled to reciprocate the stare. Then it stepped back into the pines and disappeared.

Sequoia craned his neck to see where the figure went, an uncomfortable tightness in his lungs. But it was gone. For the briefest of instants the emotion of that horrible Keeley Cure dream returned, a fist driven into his diaphragm, and the sun and the light and everything pulsed an eerie violet. It had felt so real, losing Anna that second time when he woke from the dream in the boat, a torment so unbearable his knees wanted to give out.

He took a deep breath and asked, if only he could hold it and dive down and see as a fish sees, what lay underneath the ten-thousand pieces of a broken mirror surrounding Todeket. What place had mercy here? Where was mercy, he wondered, for the smallpox victims lying sick with fever—assuming they ever existed. Or everyone who'd ever drowned here. Or mercy for Rachel Leeds. Or Jacob Wescott. This island hated mercy, in all its forms. That poor girl.

With a final unsuccessful glance toward the trees, Sequoia retraced his steps to the dock where the launch would ferry him to town and the train station and New York.

It approached at a crawl. Sequoia scolded the ferryman for his economy with the coal.

13

In her room Lisette continued packing to leave Todeket, filling the many trunks and cases with her summer wardrobe. A boy appeared in the doorway, holding the jamb, and stared at her, which she knew was his bid for attention.

She stopped and addressed him, hands on her hips. "You're here for your things, I take it?"

Eli nodded.

"Have you packed all your clothes like I asked you?"

He nodded again.

"*All* of them?"

A nod.

"And you've helped your sister pack her belongings too?"

Two quick nods, as if remembering something distasteful.

"Then you may draw awhile," said Lisette. "Go ahead and get your instruments."

As she returned to her stowing, Eli hurried to her desk, lifted up the rolltop hood, and withdrew several sheets of writing paper and a fistful of colored pencils. He carefully lowered the hood, then, as fast as he could without running—his mother would nag him if he ran—he left the room.

In the parlor, he laid a sheet of paper on the table and sat before it, waiting. His sister Sophia dashed into the room, clutching a doll. Eli scowled at her.

"Eli's writing again," she said, as if to warn the household.

A low growl escaped the boy's throat and he made a sudden move as if to leap from his seat and grab her. The girl squealed and fled.

Restored again to his loneliness, Eli focused on the blank sheet of paper. Gradually, like the rumbling of a distant storm, a very slight tremor seized his limbs. His shaking hand reached out and picked among the pencils, choosing one at random, burgundy colored. The trembling increased and his jaw fell slack.

His eyes rolled back, his hand moved toward the paper, and the pencil began to scratch across its surface.

ACKNOWLEDGMENTS

Readers wishing to learn more about the Thimble Islands are encouraged to visit the village of Stony Creek in Branford, Connecticut, to see the islands for themselves. I am indebted to Archibald Hanna's *A Brief History of the Thimble Islands in Branford, Connecticut* (1970) as well as the staff of the Stony Creek Museum for their knowledge of the Thimbles' history.

G.J.A. O'Toole's *The Spanish War: An American Epic, 1898* (1984) is an authoritative history of an overlooked war. The writings of Emanuel Swedenborg are in the public domain and available online. The stanza recited by Mr. Burke is from John Milton's *Paradise Lost* (1667).

Finally, none of my books would be possible without the support and encouragement of my wife, Kristie, our sons, James and John, and my brother, Lester, and his family. A big thank you to Eric Kurzenberger for our paddleboard excursions around the Thimbles, to Daniel Altiere for his encouragement, and to the members of the Connecticut chapter of the Horror Writers Association.